Seeking Sir Gwain

by

Shari Dare

Published by
Melange Books, LLC
White Bear Lake, MN 55110
www.melange-books.com

For everyone who wonders if love can survive between the past and the future.

Chapter One

Keith Fletcher paced the great room of his manor. It was true he was an old man. At the age of sixty, he'd fathered three children, the first of these when he was a lad of sixteen and his wife, Mary Kate, was fourteen. Their daughter Morna had been the light of their lives, but their sons, Gavin and Jon, had not lived past their fifth birthdays.

The closest thing he had to a son was his sister's youngest, Gwain McGowan. At the age of six, he had been fostered into Keith's care. Gwain had become the son Keith had been denied over the years. Even Mary Kate came to love the boy as her own. They had both agreed that he would be the heir to the estates.

How could things have changed so drastically over the years? It had all started in 1768 when Gwain's older brother called him home. Three years later, the lad returned to Fletcher Manor and announced he wanted to give up his inheritance to go in search of the woman who had captured his heart.

In a story that was too strange to believe, Gwain had been asked to father a son for his brother and then leave, never to see the boy again. It was hard for Keith to believe that his other nephew, Charles, now preferred the company of men to that of women, and he grieved for the young wife who Gwain had serviced and given a son.

Even more bizarre was that he had learned from Gwain the woman he had fallen in love with was a time traveler from a far distant twenty-first century. From what Gwain told him, the woman who was to be

1

Charles' wife had begged an old crone to allow her to change places with a future incarnation. Once she did, it was that woman who graced Gwain's bed and stole his heart.

When Gwain left on his quest to find the woman who had returned to her own time, leaving the real Davida to raise her child, Keith had finished the needed paperwork to make his grandson, Jamie, his legal heir. Now, the boy was old enough to accept his inheritance and take over the running of Fletcher Manor.

"What weighs so heavily on your mind, Keith?" Athena, the woman he had bought from a slaver so many years ago, asked.

"My thoughts have been filled with Gwain of late," Keith admitted. "I feel the need to find the lad and assure myself that the life he has chosen is fulfilling for him."

"But how can you find him? You told me that he went in search of the old crone who could send him into the future."

"So I did. I have located the old woman and she has told me of how she sent him into the future to find the woman who is there called Denise. I have offered her a king's ransom in gold to send me there as well."

The look on Athena's face was one of sorrow. "You are planning to leave me behind, aren't you? What will become of me?"

Keith took his lover in his arms. "You know that you have given me more pleasure than anyone other than my dear wife. The time you spent within the harem of a rich man of the eastern lands has served you well. You are still young enough to do whatever it is you want with your life. I have purchased you a fine house in the Inverness, where you can do whatever you wish. I have long known of your secret wish to be able to train young women in the fine art of lovemaking."

"I wouldn't even know where to start such a venture."

"I've thought of that as well. After speaking with several influential men, I have taken care of that for you. There are many men who would like to come to such a school with their young wives. Not only would the women be trained, but also the men. You will be able to teach them how to love each other. There are even men who are willing to send their sons to you to be trained in the same way as you have trained Gwain. You will make a good living for many years, as you are still a young and beautiful woman."

Athena hugged him tightly. "This is, indeed, something I have always longed for. I thank you for making my dream come true. Before you leave on your quest, I would like to give you a parting gift. Tonight will be our last together and I plan to make it most memorable for both of us." She slipped her hand, expertly, beneath his kilt and grasped his cock tightly. As though he was a prize stallion, she led him from the great room to the bedchamber where they would spend a delightful evening.

Once they were out of sight and into the darkened hall, she boldly removed her hand from his cock to caress his balls. The action prompted him to pull her into his arms. Beneath her plaid, he found the swell of her breast and pinched the nipple in anticipation of the delights that would be forthcoming once they were in his bed.

Keith enjoyed the attentions she was giving him so much he swept her into his arms to carry her to the room where they had shared pleasures for the past fifteen years. She had been a young girl of but twenty when he first purchased her. After granting her freedom, he had enjoyed many hours of delightful lovemaking. She had also trained Gwain to be the lover who was able to give such great pleasure to Charles' wife and leave her with the child Charles desired.

As soon as they entered the bedchamber, Keith knew that Athena had planned tonight in advance. A tub of steaming water sat in front of the hearth where a fire blazed in the grate.

"Tonight, I will be your love slave," Athena announced, once he set her on her feet. As soon as he did, she began removing his clothing.

As she ran her hands over his broad chest, he could feel his cock begin to swell in anticipation of the lovemaking to come. When he stood naked in front of her, she took off her clothing and the two of them stepped into the tub together. Once he seated himself in the water, Athena slid onto his lap, sending his cock into the depth of her cunt.

Sitting there, impaled, she began to kiss him and manipulate his male nipples while he grew even larger within her body. When she was satisfied with his growth, she began to move up and down, imitating the movement of when he made delightful love to her in the big bed that sat across the room from the tub.

He was about ready to spill his seed into the folds of her body when she pulled back abruptly.

"Do you mean to drive me mad, woman?"

"You will have your release, but first we will bathe and then continue our lovemaking in the bed that has given us both such delightful pleasures over the years."

Keith allowed her to wash his body while he explored hers with his fingers. In all his life he had never found a woman with such a large clit. In the past he had manipulated it between his fingers and sucked it as often as he had sucked on her nipples. He had never been disappointed because her pussy lips had always wept sweet nectar.

With their bath finished, they dried each other with the soft clothes that had been left to heat on a small chair beside the hearth. Once the last droplets of water dried, she again took his cock in her hands and led him to the bed.

He expected her to lie down on the bed and open herself to him. Instead, she insisted he lay on his back and open his legs to give her complete access to his cock. Once he was positioned to her satisfaction, she straddled him with her ass to his face and her clit within easy reach of his mouth.

Immediately, her sweet essence filled his mouth and the way she sucked his cock brought him to the brink of ejaculation. When he came, she greedily swallowed his cum as though it was the sweetest cream she had ever tasted. Unfortunately, she had left him drained and the anticipation of delightful lovemaking throughout the night seemed a distant memory.

Instead of getting up, she began to suck on his balls while he put his fingers within the folds of her cunt, while his thumb caressed her clit. Again, he began to grow as though he had become a young man driven by the urges of his sex. "What are you doing to me, woman?" he demanded. "Are you trying to kill me?"

She released his balls from her lips and he removed his fingers from within her body. "I am only making certain you are as ready for me as I am for you. When we are finished, I will tell you of the life I lived within the harem and how I learned to suck a man's balls until he cries for mercy."

Even as Keith assumed a more conventional position and began to fuck Athena with the exuberance of a man half his age, he wondered what she would tell him once he had drained them both with the night of lovemaking that lay ahead of them. He had often wondered about the life she had led in the harem but had never asked.

She said that someday she would tell him all he wanted to know, but that someday seemed far in the future. Now, with him about to embark upon a journey that would taken him hundreds of years into the future and Athena standing on the brink of a new career, someday had finally come.

The first light of dawn had just streaked across the eastern sky when Keith and Athena lay together in each other's arms. They were both spent, having made love in many different positions throughout the night.

Instead of Keith cleansing Athena, she had done so for him. As they lay together in the afterglow, he waited for Athena to tell him the things she had promised.

"I was but an infant when I was taken to the house of a known prostitute. My mother was a servant in the home of a high-ranking official and became pregnant with his child. When I was born, he refused to acknowledge a girl child and insisted that she destroy me. She was unable to do such a thing, so she took me to the house of the prostitute instead. By the time I was nine-years-old, I had been well trained and was sold to the man whose family sold me to the slaver where you found me. He was visiting the city where we lived and saw me in her house. When he asked to buy me, she set the price high in order to give my mother some money and have much of the sale price for her own pockets.

"While I was in my master's house, I learned many more ways of love, even though I wasn't allowed to lose my virginity until I became a woman. One of the things I learned to do well was to suck a man's balls until he cried for mercy. This was what was done before the master would make young male slaves into eunuchs to serve in the harem without lusting after what they were not allowed to have.

"These men would be tied to a bed and I would be brought in to suck their balls until their erections were so large that they came all over themselves. Once they did, I licked the cum from their bodies while the master had them castrated. Mine was the only sexual pleasure they would ever know."

Keith cringed at her description of what was done to these young slaves. It must have been horrible for her to witness something like this at such a young age. He thought of the horses he had gelded—to take them from wild and unpredictable stallions to gentle geldings suitable to be ridden and enjoyed. To have the same done to a man was unthinkable, and yet this was exactly what had taken place.

"I wish I could make those terrible memories disappear completely," Keith said as he pulled her into a tight embrace.

"You have allowed me to put them in the back of my mind. It was a good thing that my master died a young man. I worried what would happen to me once they put me on the auction. Luckily, you were in the market that day and bought me. I must admit I worried about what would happen to me once I left the Arab lands and came with you, but you were my master and it was not for me to question your intentions. You have made my life worth living and I thank you, not only for my freedom, but for the first time in my life, you have shown me love, and I am confident that the rest of my life will be one of great fulfillment."

Keith fell asleep holding Athena in his tight embrace. He dreamed of the day he had seen her on the auction block. He had recently become a widower and insisted on taking his shipment of wool to the Arab lands rather than entrust it to a broker. He had wanted adventure and instead he found a beautiful woman in chains. Unable to leave her there, he took the money he had gotten from the sale of his wool and purchased her. He knew she would fill the void left by Mary Kate's death. She and she alone would breathe life into the manor house.

Chapter Two

Ian Brice walked the cold streets of Inverness. The icy wind blew in from the north, causing him to pull his cloak closer around his neck. The wool from the sheep of his cousin, William McGowen, as well as the other clans around the area, had been brought into his warehouse and stood ready for the auction. With the change in the weather, the pounds of wool that would be sold at auction would be taken by ship from his warehouse to England, as well as various ports on the continent.

At times like these, he envied his cousin. William only had to relax in front of a roaring fire and reap the fruit of his labor until winter let go of its icy grip.

"Ian!"

He looked to his left to see who had called his name. He smiled as the woman who graced his bed last night waved at him. For someone who had given him so much pleasure just a few short hours ago, she certainly looked as though she was well rested. She was the wife of a wealthy man who was much older than she, and he had paid Ian well to get his young bride with child. It was something he'd done for many well-to-do families, when the husband was unable to carry out his duties and give his wife a child. The practice certainly lined his pockets and gave him a variety of women to enjoy.

As he thought about these women, his cousin William came to mind. William was just as lusty as Ian. His first wife had given him two healthy children, but died along with the child while giving birth to the third. It had taken William little time to remarry and his second wife, Lorna, had given him four children in the span of five years. They'd been very happy together, but Ian couldn't help wondering if his cousin tired of being tied to one wife and raising six children.

Of course, raising children didn't come easily to Ian, perhaps because he'd been fostered to Charles McGowen at such an early age. His father, Lachlan Brice, had insisted that his youngest son be fostered away from Brice Manor. It was convenient that his cousin Davida had married Charles just two years earlier, giving Lachlan the ability to have his youngest son fostered far from home in the highlands.

Years later, Ian met his older brother Kyle and had been told that the real reason for his exile was that their father suspected their mother of whoring herself to one of the young crofters, and that Ian had been the product of that union. It was no wonder his father wanted nothing to do with him. After learning the truth, he had not even tried to contact his other brother, Father Evan. There had to be a reason, other than that it was expected of him, for a man like Evan Brice to become a priest. The same blood flowed through Evan's veins that ran through Ian's and Kyle's, therefore, it was unthinkable that he would willingly agree to a life without sex.

The role of surrogate father, which Ian portrayed so easily, was much different. The men who would become the true fathers to the sons and daughters he had planted within their mother's bodies paid him handsomely for his services. It was no different than when he sold the services of his stallions as studs for various lords in and around Inverness.

He'd been but three years old when his father sent him to McGowen Manor. Only one year older than William, they became fast friends. He was six when Charles had been murdered and Angus took his anger out on Brian. It was common knowledge that Brian had killed Charles in a jealous lover's quarrel, but as Ian grew older, he wondered if that were really the truth of the matter. It was entirely possible that the deed had been the work of Charles' lovely wife, Davida. Even as a child, Ian could see how his father's cousin had suffered as Charles' wife. It was no secret that Charles spent his nights in the same chamber as Brian and often degraded his wife in front of the entire clan.

Seeking Sir Gwain

After the murder, Ian had begged his father to allow him to return home, but instead Angus McGowen had become his foster father and taught him the things he would need to survive as a grown man, without acreage or monies from his father.

It was Angus who had insisted that Ian learn the business of buying and selling wool and instructed him in the many ways to pleasure a woman. It all began with Bonnie, the daughter of one of the crofters. She had been his first conquest and when she became pregnant with his child, her father quickly married her off to a neighbor's son whom he held responsible.

Ian hadn't argued. He wanted no part of fatherhood. He'd been in Inverness for less than a year when a merchant who had a shop not far from Ian's office approached him. When he agreed to give the older man's young wife a child, **he** found himself beginning what had become a profitable business over the years. Many of the children of the elite of Inverness belonged to him and the majority of them were boys. He was paid handsomely for his services. It didn't matter that these men saved him many coins from his purse since he no longer had to visit the whores who plied their trade along the wharf. He was doing them a service and one for which he was well paid.

Ahead of him, he saw the silhouette of a man standing outside the door to his office. From behind he couldn't tell if the man was someone out to rob him of his purse, a prospective buyer for his wool, or a friend come for a visit. Due to the cold, the man was wrapped in a cloak of dark wool, obscuring his features from Ian's view. Rather than take chances, he gripped the handle of his knife so that he would be prepared for an unprovoked attack.

* * * *

William had arrived in Inverness late the previous evening. The reason for his journey came to light shortly after his mother's death. It had taken him the better part of a month to make the decision to beg Ian to help him find the man who fathered him.

With each mile that his horse traversed, he recalled the words of the letter he'd found among his mother's possessions after her death.

My dear son,

When I am gone, there is no reason why you cannot know of the situation surrounding your birth. I was to wed another, but the soothsayer said that my lover would be killed and I would be given as bride to Charles. The thought of it was overwhelming, so I pleaded with her to allow me to change places with a future incarnation of my spirit.

She granted my wish, but I knew all of what transpired while I was far in the future. Charles did not consummate the marriage on their wedding night, nor did he do so when they arrived at McGowen Manor. That became the duty of your real father, Gwain.

Once you were born, I ached to hold you in my arms and begged to be returned to my own time. I had no idea that my husband would not come to my bed, but as time went on I became so lonely, I wished for a lover. I killed Charles one night after drinking far too much wine and walking in on Charles and Brian as they made love. Once I did, I made certain that everyone thought the murderer was Brian. Angus took care of the rest.

I have no remorse for what I did, for it was evil for Charles to be with Brian as if he were a woman, while he left me wanting in my chamber.

My wish is for you to find your true father. The old soothsayer is Tabitha. It has been said that she left shortly after Gwain disappeared, went to Kyle of Lochlash, and from there secluded herself on the Isle of Syke.

I beg you to find her and insist she tell you where your father had gone, for I know in my heart of hearts that she had something to do with his disappearance.

Upon his arrival, William hesitated going to his cousin's house so late at night. It was possible that he was entertaining one of the many women who came to him hoping to have a child for their aging husbands. Instead he had found lodging at the home of one of the most famous Madams in the city, a woman by the name of Athena. On other occasions, he had visited her home and paid more than a night's lodging to enjoy the pleasures of the young women who didn't care that he was the head of his clan or that he had a wife and six children at home.

By the light of day, his cock felt warm and well satisfied, even though the rest of his body shook with the damp cold of the wind that seemed to blow incessantly. He'd been a fool to make this trip in winter when the heavy snows in the highlands were deep and the wind blew cold and fierce from the north.

"Are you waiting for me?" Ian's voice warmed William with the promise of a warm fire and perhaps a drop of whiskey once they were inside the office.

"I was waiting for my cousin, Ian, the man who opens his business promptly at seven each morning. It is well past eight and he has yet to open the door, but I suppose you will do even if you are a poor substitute."

Ian slapped him on the back and hurried to unlock the door to the office. Upon entering, the warmth of the room embraced him.

"How do you manage to keep this room warm, even after you have been away for the night?" William asked.

"I hire a man to come in before seven and bank the fires. That way when I arrive, the office is as warm as I want it to be. I doubt you came here to inquire about the warmth of my office. What is it that brings you away from the comfort of your manor, to say nothing of the bed of your lovely wife?"

"I have come on a fool's mission, but perhaps if we have a drop of the whiskey I know you keep locked away from your employees, it won't seem so foolish."

Ian opened the cupboard and produced a bottle of fine whiskey along with two glasses. Once he had poured each of them a generous portion, he sat down in his chair and propped his feet upon the desk.

"Now cousin, what is this mission that brings you from the highlands to Inverness?"

"As you recall, I sent you word of my mother's passing. After her death I found this letter among her possessions."

Ian took the letter and scanned the contents. "With the exception of the part about her changing places with a future incarnation, there is nothing in this letter I didn't already know or at least suspect."

"Are you telling me you knew that Charles wasn't my father and that my mother was the one who killed him?"

"In respect to your parentage, it was Angus who told me the truth when I was ready to embark on my adult life and become a surrogate father for the old men of Inverness as well as many other places. He told me not to make the same mistake as your sire and fall in love with the women I was bedding. He said that on your naming day, Gwain was banned from McGowen Manor. The story is that he returned to the home of his uncle who had fostered him and from there disappeared, never to be heard from again. As for your mother killing Charles, I don't blame her. I was older and saw more than they thought I did. No man should ever treat his wife the way he treated her, nor should he keep his lover, male or female, under the same roof. Affairs like the one carried out by Charles and Brian should be kept private. When I am paid to bed a woman, her husband's servants bring her to my home. Never once do I defile a man's home by invading it. That, I am afraid, is exactly what Brian did, when Charles moved him to McGowen Manor. He defiled the home where Davida was brought to become the mistress of the house."

"Will you help me?" William asked.

"Do you mean will I go to the Isle of Skye and look for this woman?"

"Exactly. I have duties that keep me with the clan, but with the winter setting in you have to store the wool you have purchased for the ships that will be coming in the spring. It would not take that long to find this Tabitha and persuade her to tell you where you can find my father."

Ian took a long drink from the glass of whiskey and stared into the fire, as though contemplating William's suggestion. "The Isle of Skye is a wild and foreboding place, especially during the winter. What will be my compensation for such a journey?"

Ian watched as William contemplated what he could offer as compensation. "That is a difficult question to answer. I could offer you money, but I know you have more of that than you can ever hope to spend. If I were to offer you land, you would scoff at me. I know that you are well pleased with your life here in Inverness. That leaves women. There are many fair maidens among the families of the clan, but I know you well enough to understand that you would never be content with just one woman in your bed. What I can offer you is the adventure of such a mission and the hope to find the man who did for my mother what you have done for so many women in the past."

Ian chuckled. "You know me far too well, cousin. The adventure is worth the inconvenience of traveling to the Isle of Skye. Give me a few days to get my affairs in order and I will do this for you."

William smiled for the first time. Ian had known the truth about William's parents for years, but never said anything. Yet, hearing everything that had been whispered within the confines of McGowan Manor confirmed had been enough to make him feel like someone had punched him in the stomach.

* * * *

William stayed with Ian for several days, helping him make arrangements for his businesses. Many of the men whom he had helped in the past with their young wives were irate at the thought that Ian was leaving the city for an indefinite period of time. To ease their minds, he turned the business over to Sean MacGinnis, the man who had helped him manage the business for several years.

Finally, everything was in place and the two cousins parted company. While William went back to the highlands, Ian headed north. He took a coach as far as possible and finally found someone with a boat who would take him to the Isle of Skye.

"Do you know anything about an old crone by the name of Tabitha?" he asked as they fought the wind to maneuver the ice-crusted water that separated the mainland from the island.

"She is well known for her ability to predict the future. People say that she is able to send someone to either the past or the future, although I don't believe such nonsense. No one can change the time in which a man lives. For that matter, who would want to do such a thing?"

It is possible that I would want to do this. If Gwain disappeared completely, perhaps he followed the incarnation of Davida, who was

13

taken from him after the birth of their son. This might be more of an adventure than I first thought it would be.

The man left him on the shore after giving him directions to where he could rent a horse and get more details about Tabitha's home.

At the stable, the man warned him not to go to Tabitha's cottage. "Ye would be smart to turn back now, laddie. That woman is well versed in black magic. They say she is hundreds of years old and her predictions usually come true. As a God-fearing man, I keep my distance from the old hag. It is said that she can easily turn a man's cock to jelly, making him incapable of giving a woman pleasure. Ye are much too young to have such a thing happen to you."

Ian laughed at the man's concern. "I've come a long way to find her. It has been a difficult journey. I doubt that there is anything she can do to cause me harm. I do not believe that even an old hag like Tabitha is capable of rendering a man unable to perform with a woman. I thank you for the information and the rental of the horse."

He rode through the countryside, pleased with the break in the weather. The breezes from the ocean were almost balmy, and the weak winter sun made the snow glisten as though it were strewn with diamonds.

"It took you long enough to get here," the old woman said when she answered the door.

"You knew I was coming?" he asked.

"Aye, I knew and I have prepared for you. I know it has been a long time since you have had a woman so I have a willing partner waiting for you. Her husband is unable to get her with child due to his advanced age. I told him of your coming and he paid me well for you to bed the lass and get her with a child. It will take you but one try, but I am certain you will enjoy her more times than that while you are here."

"If you knew I was coming, old woman, do you know why I have come as well?"

"You know I do, but I don't think you are ready for what I have to tell you. Before we begin, come in and warm yourself by my fire. I have a fine stew simmering on the fire and a long story to tell you. When I finish, if you still want to pursue this mission, you will embark on an adventure from which there will be no return."

Ian wondered what the old woman meant, but knew she would tell him everything he wanted to know in due time. Instead of pressing her further, he accepted the food and comfort that she offered him and seated himself in one of the chairs that graced her cottage.

"It was many years ago when the young Davida first came to me," she said, once she filled her own bowl. "She was to marry a man by the name of Robert whom she loved with all her heart, but I saw his death and learned that he would be replaced by Charles McGowan as her husband. She had heard of Charles and decided that she didn't want to marry him. It was well known that he was a cruel man and possibly a lover who took his own pleasure at the expense of the woman, both mentally and physically. She pleaded with me to change her destiny. The only thing I could do was to bring a future incarnation of her soul to take her place. She hated it in the future, but once the child was born, she ached to hold the lad in her arms. I brought her back so that she could raise her son."

"What I want to know is what happened to Gwain?"

"Do not rush me, young man. I told Gwain the truth and he knew on the naming day of his son that the Davida he knew and loved had returned to the future. After he left McGowan Manor, it took him several months to find me, but when he did, he insisted I send him to the future in search of the woman who had stolen his heart. I told him that if I sent him there, he would no longer be a young man. He would be a bit older than her, but I would allow him to take his riches so that he could live comfortably. I know that he found her and they are happy together."

Ian was intrigued by what Tabitha said. "Can you send me to the future in search of him?"

"Do you have any idea what you ask? I can easily send you forward in time. I can give you all the knowledge that you will need to live there for the remainder of your life, and I can also allow you to take your riches with you. What I cannot do is guarantee you love in the future, nor can I allow you to return to the life you have lived since leaving McGowan Manor. You will live out your life in a time and place that are unfamiliar to you. There will be many things for you to learn and many new inventions for you to become acquainted with."

"I understand. How will I know about these things?"

15

"The young woman who requires your services will be here for three months. In that time it will be confirmed that she is indeed pregnant. Once the confirmation has been made to her husband, you will be free to go into the future and embark upon the mission your cousin has sent you on. As for knowing about the future, while you are here I will impart the information you will need to know through your dreams. You will not remember any of it until you reach the future. Once you arrive there, you will know exactly what to do and say. Your name will be the same as it is now, but you will be a young man of means, one who will not have to work for a living."

The old woman turned her attention from Ian to the pot that was bubbling on the hook that was suspended over the fire blazing in the hearth. He thought about what she told him.

Will I find love in the future? And if I do, will the women who live there be like the ones I've enjoyed over the years? If they aren't, will I be able to satisfy them?

Chapter Three

"This is Ian, the man I told you about. Ian, this is Shamus MacIntyre," Tabitha said as she led an older man and his young wife into the cottage.

"Can I be assured that you will live up to all the things Tabitha has told me about you?"

Ian assessed the man who stood before him. He looked no different than any of the other men who had requested his services over the years. His stomach was fat from all the rich food he had indulged in. His overindulgence was more than likely the reason that he could no longer satisfy his young wife and give her the child he so desperately wanted.

It was possible that in time she would resent her husband for not gracing her bed. He wondered if Shamus would suffer the same fate that befell Charles McGowan.

"If you lived in Inverness, you would not ask such a foolish question, Mr. MacIntyre. My prowess with the women of that fair city is known by all and of the children I have fathered. The majority of them are male so that your name will not be lost for lack of an heir."

"Then I leave Brenna here in your care. I will return in three months to reclaim my wife. If she is indeed with child, I will reward you handsomely. If you fail, I will castrate you so that you can fool no other men in the future."

The mention of the word 'future' made Ian think about the mission he was about to embark upon. Would he be able to understand the world in which he'd be living? Should he change his mind and return to Inverness?

He knew the latter was tempting but entirely impossible. He couldn't disappoint William.

Shamus pushed Brenna into Ian's arms, before leaving the cottage. The expression on her face was one of despair.

"How could he leave me here?" she cried, before burying her face against his broad chest.

Her tears wet his shirt, but they were far from his mind. It was her breasts that caught his attention. They were small and he knew the nipples would easily pebble with his attention to them.

Earlier, Tabitha had told him that she would return to the manor with Shamus and work her magic upon his body so that he would be able to pleasure his wife. She told Ian that it was doubtful that Shamus would ever be able to father a child, since he had suffered a terrible illness during his childhood that prevented it. He did not believe her, but since his first three wives had remained childless until they met untimely deaths, it was evident that the man would remain childless without Ian's help.

With Brenna in his arms, he did not want to see her meet the same fate as her predecessors.

"You must be cold," he said, as he guided her to the fire. "Warm yourself while I prepare your bath."

"Bath!" she shrieked '"It is but mid February and much too cold for such pleasures."

"You have much to learn, my dear Brenna. I do not bed women who are not cleansed to my standards. I will see to your bath and I promise you will enjoy it. Tabitha has a massive tub that will accommodate both you and me comfortably. It is built over a hot spring and gives a body great pleasure. I have used it every day since my arrival and find I am completely refreshed and more than ready for lovemaking. Once you find how fulfilling it is, you will be able to instruct your husband on the pleasure of such a simple thing."

"It will be no use, for his cock is as soft as pudding. He has bedded me but instructed the midwife to take my virginity since he was unable to penetrate me and do so for himself. After that, he has fucked me nightly, but it is only for his pleasure. I find his visits to my bed distasteful, to say the least."

"Tabitha is working with her herbs in order to give him back his ability to make love to you satisfactorily, while I teach you the beauty of lovemaking as well as planting a child within your belly. I will finish preparing our bath while you allow the heat from the hearth to penetrate your body."

She looked at him skeptically, but did as he told her. When she finally took off the heavy cloak that had covered her body from head to toe, he could see the small breasts that he felt through the material earlier. She had a tiny waist and from what he could tell, her hips were meant for birthing babies.

He went into the bathing room and to his surprise she followed him closely. He heard her gasp at the steam that rose from the massive tub. *This will be an interesting experience for both of us.*

He had noticed earlier that she was very young. He expected her to be afraid of him, but she came willingly to his side.

"This will be our first lesson. This time I will do all the work, but in time you will learn how to give me pleasure as well."

He began by unpinning the piece of plaid that signified the colors of the MacIntyre clan. Piece by piece, he removed her clothing until at last she stood in front of him, completely naked.

"You have a beautiful body," he said, as he took her breasts in his hands. Indeed, they were small, but her nipples were larger than most and tempted him to reach out and manipulate them with his thumbs and fingers.

As he raised his gaze to her face, he saw the blush that graced her cheeks and she looked down toward the floor. "Are you embarrassed to be naked in front of me?"

Brenna nodded her head.

"You are a married woman, Brenna, how is it that you are embarrassed to be naked in front of a man?"

"I have never been naked for my husband. He prefers to have me under the covers and wearing a long sleeping gown. I have never seen him naked either. He comes to my bed in the dark and does his rutting beneath the blankets. I can only feel the softness of his cock and endure the fucking that he calls lovemaking."

"From this day forward, you will find that lovemaking is not only pleasurable, but the beauty of the human body will excite you. I will teach you everything I know, while Tabitha works her magic on your husband. If she cannot help him, she will insist that he find you a lover. Once you are satisfied, your time with your husband will be more pleasurable. There is something I would like to know. How old are you and how long have you been married to Shamus?"

She raised her head and met his gaze. "I am sixteen. On my fifteenth birthday, my older brother gave me as bride to Shamus. I am the youngest of six children. My older sister was given a good dowry while my other sister was given to the church as a nun. My older brother became lord of our manor upon our father's death, my youngest brother died as a child, and the other brother is a priest. My brother told me that I would have to marry Shamus because he desired only an alliance with our clan and not a dowry. When I asked what had happened to the dowry my father promised me, he said that as lord of the manor, he decided to use it for his daughters. I am nothing to him. He was pleased to get me out of his home and away from his children. He has no idea how miserable I am in this life as Shamus' wife. I am afraid that I will meet with an accident that will take my life if you do not get me with child before I return to MacIntyre Manor."

Instead of answering her verbally, Ian took her breasts in his large hands and began to manipulate her nipples until Brenna moaned with complete pleasure.

"You have me at an unfair advantage, my lord. I long to see the body of a young man and see what it is that men have between their legs that is supposed to give women great pleasure."

Ian smiled at Brenna's suggestion. She was a fair lass and more than willing to comply with what he would be doing to her. It was possible that a wild sexual being hid beneath the golden lashes that guarded her green eyes.

He quickly took off his clothes. Once free, his cock sprang to attention, giving credence to the fact that this woman excited him greatly.

She reached out her dainty hand to touch him, but he stopped her. "There will be time for you to find gratitude by playing with my sex, but this first encounter between the two of us is for your pleasure and your pleasure alone."

He picked up her naked body and gently deposited her into the tub of hot water. Once she was seated, he sat behind her, with his arousal sliding beneath her ass and resting against her intimate place. He picked up the soft cloth that he'd lay beside the tub and lathered it with the soap that Tabitha had given him.

He started his ministrations by washing her back and then moving his hands around to rub the cloth over her small breasts and enlarged nipples. While he did that, she relaxed against his chest and moaned with great pleasure.

As soon as he was certain that her relaxation was complete, he moved the cloth down over her belly to the tangled curls that guarded her woman's soul. He could tell that his brazenness surprised her as he felt her tense, but he continued to slip his fingers, without the cloth, across the nub of her desire. As he did, she mewed like a contented kitten. Just knowing that he could arouse her so easily, he continued his journey through the moist valley of her womanhood until her found the channel that would sheath his cock as soon as they finished with their bath. Tentatively, he slipped in one finger, followed by a second, third, and fourth. When he was certain she was ready to accommodate him completely, he finished in the tub and got out. After drying himself, he picked her up and wrapped her in a drying sheet before carrying her to his bed.

"What have you done to me?" she whispered, when he lay down beside her and again began his game of touch and play that would make her ready for his lovemaking. Again he manipulated her breasts until he decided he would rather suck her delightful nipples than continue to play with them. As he took one of them in his mouth and began to suckle, he moved his hand back to her clit. He knew it would take only a little attention to this sensitive part of her body for her to be wet and begging him to enter her in the way a man was meant to fuck a woman.

"Please Ian, please end this delightful torture. Make me a complete woman. Make love to me and give me the pleasure that I deserve."

"Anything you ask, my love," he said, as he shifted position. His cock was hard and ready for her love sheath. He knew other men would call it her cunt, but the word seemed too harsh for this beautiful woman who lay beneath him.

Knowing her husband had abused her sexually, he took things slowly. It would be like bedding a virgin. He had only been with a handful of virgins in the past, but he had learned early on that they needed love and careful caring when it came to their first sexual experience.

He could feel her fear, especially when he began to enter her body with his cock. "You really are going to fuck me," she said, her voice sounding with tears that were left unshed.

"No, my dear, I am going to make love to you. In time, I will teach you ways in which you can pleasure your husband, and how you can tell him what you want him to do for you as well. If Tabitha's herbs and potions work, it is likely that you will enjoy many years of lovemaking with your husband."

"I don't know if that is what I want. He is an old man and the fat on his belly turns my stomach. I have no desire for this lovemaking you speak of."

"Ah, my love, you will change your mind. You are young and the experience you have had is not a good one. Once you find what lovemaking can be, you will find that this is something that is not only natural, but also enjoyable. I am going to enter you now, but I promise I will go slowly. It will not be painful as I am certain it was on your wedding night, but it will be different from anything you have experienced before."

Knowing that her young body had a powerful effect on him, he gently slid his cock into her cunt. As he did, he saw a look of surprise in Brenna's eyes. It changed almost immediately to one of pleasure. Many times he brought her to the brink of climax, only to back off in order to prolong the ecstasy of their lovemaking. When he could hold back no longer, he allowed himself to spill his seed. If Tabitha could be believed, this coupling would be the beginning of a new life that would grow within Brenna's body.

This child would be yet another of his offspring that he could never claim, but for the first time it mattered more than he thought possible. Never before had he fallen in love with a woman he was bedding to give her husband a child. Brenna was beautiful and from the moment he first saw her, he knew she was going to always be a special memory in his mind. Once she went back to her husband, he would be transported to the future. He could only pray that he could find someone as special in another time and place.

* * * *

As soon as Brenna was positive that she carried Ian's child, she realized that she wanted to know more of the ways that a woman could pleasure a man. "You promised to show me how to make my husband happy in our bed. What did you mean?" she asked as she and Ian readied themselves for bed.

"I will begin by showing you a new pleasure and then you will better understand what I am talking about."

Since they had just finished their nightly bath, she was anxious for this new lesson in love. She hurried to the bed and lay down, opening herself to him. Instead of mounting her as he had so many others in the past, he knelt at the foot of the bed and opened her nether-lips wide so that he could completely gaze upon her woman parts.

"In the past, I know that you have received pleasure when I have manipulated your clit."

He reached for the nub and she moaned with the pleasure that she so enjoyed. To her disappointment, he removed his hand only to cover her clit with his lips. Immediately he began to suckle it as though he were enjoying her breasts--as if he was again a baby. The sensation that coursed through her was the most overpowering sexual experience she had enjoyed since arriving at the cottage for her time with Ian.

"Did you like what I just did to you?" he asked, just as she exploded with an orgasm. She never expected to be so aroused by anything other than Ian's physical lovemaking.

"Yes, but how did you make me cum for you without ever entering me?"

"There are many ways for a man to pleasure a woman without actually making love to her. It is the same for a woman. What I am going to ask of you now is something you might find repulsive at first, but in time you will learn to enjoy it as much as your husband will. The thing I will instruct you to do is something that will make me cum without entering you. It will take practice, but you will find it is best if you will be able to swallow that which comes from my body and fills your mouth. Your essence is sweet to me, and I pray you will feel the same about my cum."

Terror filled Brenna's mind. She had seen Ian's cock numerous times over the past weeks. She knew what it could do when he put it in her cunt. What she didn't know was that she could also put it in her mouth. The thought, although slightly repulsive, was at the same time exciting.

She watched as he lay down beside her on the bed. For the first time, she tentatively traced her fingers down the length of his cock. It felt as velvety to her touch as it did when it slipped into her woman's folds. Even with the smooth skin, she was intrigued with the hardness of this appendage. Unable to stop herself, she wrapped her fingers around it. It pulsed beneath her hand, causing her to pull back.

"Have I hurt you?"

Ian laughed. "On the contrary, you have given me great pleasure. Now is when we will play a game of pretense. You will pretend that your mouth is your cunt. If that is the case, slide the length of me into your mouth."

Her initial repulsion was overshadowed by the memory of the pleasure she'd received when Ian had sucked on her clit. If it was possible for her to give him the same extent of pleasure, she knew it was what must be done. Puckering her lips, she slid across his thick shaft, allowing it to become completely encased through her lips and inside her mouth.

Quite unsure of what to do next, she began to move up and down on his cock to imitate the act of intercourse. It hardly seemed possible, but he became even harder than he had been when she first started her ministrations.

"Are you certain you have never done this before, Brenna?" Ian groaned.

She allowed the head of his cock to slip from her lips. "I have never done such a thing before, Ian. Why do you ask?"

"Because you are as adept as any of the street women in Inverness. It matters not how you know what to do. I am more than happy to be the recipient of your attentions."

She smiled. Even though she had never done this before, she found it came easily for her. Once she again started moving up and down on his cock, she moved her fingers around the base of his shaft. She moved her hand back to the two sacks behind his cock and to her surprise, they were even more velvety but not as hard. Within each sack was a ball that she was able to roll around with very little effort.

"What are you doing to me, woman?" he asked.

She could tell that he was completely at her mercy. She imprisoned his cock within the confines of his mouth and by her gentle manipulation of his balls, she was able to make him moan with pleasure. She wondered if she would be able to do such things to her husband. Certainly, he must have balls behind his cock the same way that Ian did.

In the year that she'd been married, she had never seen her husband naked. He had come to her by the dark of night and slipped beneath the covers. Then and only then did he pull up his nightshirt and proceed to try and put his soft cock into her body. Once she returned to the manor, she would certainly look at his cock and check to see if he had the balls that were so much fun to play with. Even if he wasn't able to give her a child, it was possible that with Tabitha's miracle herbs he may be able to give her much pleasure.

As she continued to manipulate Ian's balls, she could feel his cock pulse within her mouth. Only moments later he came in her mouth. True to his prediction, she enjoyed the taste of his cum as she allowed it to slide down her throat. Almost instantly, his cock relaxed, indicating that it wouldn't be ready to enter her again until he had time to recover.

Unwilling to give up her new toy, she moved her mouth to his balls and began to suck, first on one and then the other. While she did, she caressed his cock with her hand and began to move the foreskin up and down in a rhythm that mirrored the way she was sucking.

It took only moments for him to become hard enough to make love to her. "You are wicked, Brenna MacIntyre. For the delightful punishment you have given me, prepare to be punished in the same way."

"Punishment? I know nothing of what you speak."

"You are a sassy wench. What you have been doing to me is a pleasant torture. It is not that I am complaining, but you have had enough lessons in pleasuring a man on this day. Now it is my turn to teach you a lesson in sexual torture. I want you to get on your hands and knees, with your ass facing me."

The expression on Brenna's face was one of bewilderment. "Why would you want my ass in your face?"

"Believe me, love, it will not be in my face."

She did as he said and he mounted her as a stallion would mount a mare. In the process, he shoved his cock deep into her cunt, making her shriek with pleasure at this way of making love. As much as he wanted to play with her tits that hung like play toys from her body, he refrained. He knew that when a woman carried a man's child within her belly, her breasts were tender, and to play with them would bring great discomfort. The last thing he ever wanted to do was to make this woman uncomfortable.

* * * *

It hardly seemed as though three months had passed, but on a sunny day in May, Shamus and Tabitha returned to the cottage. Shamus' appearance came as a shock. His body looked as though he were a much younger man. The fat that had hung from his belly and jowls was replaced with toned muscle. It was apparent that Tabitha had worked her magic with spells as well as with herbs.

"Is my wife carrying a child?" Shamus asked, his hand resting on the knife that was sheathed on the belt that girded his waist.

"She is with child," Ian declared.

"I see no bulge in her belly. How can I be certain that you tell me the truth?"

"Since my arrival, I have not had my monthly flow and my breasts are tender," Brenna replied. "I am also sick every morning, although that is coming to an end. I go several days in a row without having to use the chamber pot upon waking. The reason you do not see the bulge of my belly is because my clothing covers it. Already I can see evidence of the child growing beneath my heart."

Shamus began to smile, but it was Tabitha who laughed out loud. "There is more than one child growing beneath your heart, Brenna," she said. "You will give birth to healthy twin sons. They will be the children of your old age, Shamus. I say such a gift is well worth the monies you have promised to Ian. In addition, the changes I have helped you make in your life will keep your wife happy in your bed. Through my herbs and magic, you will again be able to bed your wife with the lust and vigor of a man half your age."

Brenna smiled. Ian knew that she would use all the sexual tricks he had introduced her to in order to keep her husband happy for years to come.

"It is time for you to leave, my love," he said, as he took her in his arms one last time and kissed her farewell.

"Yes Ian, it is time for me to show my husband the pleasures you have taught me. I have taken your lessons to heart. From now on my husband will not be disappointed in either his nights in our bed or the twins that Tabitha has predicted we will have."

Shamus handed Ian a bag of gold before taking his wife back to MacIntyre Manor. Ian watched them leave with the tug of regret on his heart. Never before had he been the constant companion for the women he bedded for three months. He would miss Brenna, but the promise of adventure that awaited him in the future pulled him like a magnet.

"Are you ready for your journey?" Tabitha asked.

"The dreams you have given me, if indeed they have existed, are not foremost in my mind, but I have delayed too long in granting the wishes of my cousin William."

Tabitha nodded. "In the future, you will be a man of means. The gold that Shamus gave you, as well as the fortune you have within the vaults of the bank in Inverness, will be transferred to accounts in your name in the town of Minter, Wisconsin. That is where you will begin your life as a man of means in the future. You must use what is called the "lonely hearts" column to find a woman who will lead you to Gwain. The woman you find will be older, but she will be appreciative of your expertise in lovemaking. Tonight you will go to bed in this cottage, but when you wake, you will be in your flat in the twenty-first century. All the arrangements have been made and your future is secure. You are embarking upon a great adventure. I know that you are man enough to accept the challenge and make the woman who will be in your life as happy as you have made Shamus and Brenna."

Darkness was falling and as it did, Ian prepared to go to the bed that seemed so empty--to dream of the future that was five hundred years away from everything he had ever known.

Chapter Four

Minter, Wisconsin 2008

Keith awoke in a strange bed. Sitting at his side was a man he didn't recognize. "Who are you?" Keith asked.

"It matters not who I am. Like you, I am a time traveler, and I know of Tabitha and those like her who have sent us into the future to find that which we seek. I have made all the arrangements for the life you will live in this time and place. The education that I will give you will be invaluable since another will come in search of the man, Gwain. His name will be Ian Brice, and he will be the fosterling of Charles McGowan. He has come on this adventure to find the man who fathered William McGowan and tell him of his son."

Keith was confused but he listened intently as the man told him of the life he would be living and the things he would find in this exciting new world of the future.

* * * *

Ian awoke to find he slept in a bed that wasn't nearly as soft as a feather bed, but softer than the straw pallet he'd occupied at Tabitha's cottage. To his surprise, he wore nothing beneath the crisp sheets, not even a nightshirt like the ones he'd worn all his life. His cock felt full, but he knew it wasn't because of desire. It was the usual feeling he had when he needed to relieve himself in the chamber pot.

Rather than contemplate his physical need, he opened his eyes. If Tabitha was right, he would find himself in a flat in the twenty-first century where he could begin his search for the elusive Gwain.

Without dressing, he got out of bed and went in search of either a chamber pot or a privy where he would take care of his morning duties before starting his search in earnest.

The flat he now occupied was more elegant than anywhere he had ever lived. The windows let in the morning sunlight and beneath his feet was a thick carpet that rivaled even those made of skins in the finest houses in Inverness. It was certainly different from the rushes that covered the floors at McGowan Manor. The furnishings, too, were different from any he had ever seen. The bed was high off the floor, not because it sat on a raised platform, but because beneath the thick mattress was a box-like thing that was covered with fabric. It was also the largest bed he had even seen. Across the room was another piece of furniture with a large mirror over it.

Although his hair was mussed from sleep, he looked no different than he had just one day earlier. Running his hand over the stubble on his cheek, he realized that he needed his morning shave. When he had gone on his quest to find Tabitha, he had given up going to his favorite barber for this one particular indulgence. It had been an extravagance he had learned to enjoy, but knew he could do without.

Tabitha's promise that he would know everything he needed to know when he awakened came true. Looking around the room, he realized that the piece of furniture with the mirror was called a dresser, the bed was considered king-sized, the chest across the room was called a chest of drawers, and behind the door in the corner he would find a closet, complete with clothing for him to wear.

"I thought you'd never get up," an older man said, when Ian walked out of the room. "I certainly expected you to put on some clothes before leaving the bedroom. You've been sleeping for two days. Of course I did the same thing when Tabitha first brought me through time."

For the first time, Ian was embarrassed by his nudity in front of this stranger. "W–who are you?"

"I am Keith Fletcher, Gwain's uncle. I came forward in time in search of my nephew. Tabitha has communicated to me that you are in search of the same man."

Ian took a moment to assess the older man who sat in an overstuffed chair watching him. "How long have you been here?"

"It was 1475 when I went to Tabitha and begged her to help me find Gwain. She finally agreed and I have been here for about a month acclimating myself to the new surroundings. Several days ago, she came to me in a dream and told me of your desire to find Gwain as well. I have been preparing for your arrival."

"I don't understand. It was 1508 when I left. How is it that you came thirty-three years prior to me, yet you've only been here for one month?"

"Time travel is a strange thing. Tabitha told me that a man could be sent to any period in time. She told me that the time she was sending me to would be within a year of Gwain's arrival. If she's right, I will find him soon."

"How is it that you live in such luxury?"

"Tabitha transferred my fortune to a bank here in the future. She also arranged for all the proper paperwork for me to live legally in this time and place. She has done the same for you and the two of us will be living as fine gentlemen of means. I will be telling everyone that you are my nephew and have just arrived from Scotland. With the gold that was transferred here, I am independently wealthy, and you are as well."

"This is a magnificent flat."

"Here they are not called flats. They are called condos. Rather than renting accommodations, you own this one. I own one that is next door, but of course, since you came to this time and place, I have been staying here so that you would not awaken alone. With living accommodations such as these, there are servants who come and take care of the gardens. I am told they also remove the snow that falls in the winter."

"Why would anyone remove the snow?"

"I am told that life is different here. Winter is not a time of rest, as it is for us. Here, people do not let the snow keep them prisoner within their homes. They go about their daily routines and expect the snow to be removed promptly. It is a strange custom, but you will find there are many strange customs within this time period."

"Since you have been here longer than I, have you found Gwain?"

"Not yet, since I have been spending my time here learning the best way to start. I have found a wonderful thing called the 'personals' column in the daily newspaper. I decided it best if we advertise for women who would be of the same age as Denise, the woman who Gwain decided to follow to the future."

"This is indeed a different time from whence we came. I have never heard of anyone advertising for a woman."

"It is much different from the word of mouth that has brought women to your bed over the years. The man that Tabitha sent to educate me on how to live in the twenty-first century told me of your exploits with women and how their husbands paid you well for getting their young brides with child. Here you are free to bed a woman if that is what you wish. It is actually expected by some of the women you will be dating. I think you will fit in quite well."

As interesting as Ian found this conversation, he realized he needed to find a privy. "Where is the privy in this place?" he finally asked.

Keith smiled at the question. "Here it is called a bathroom and it's in the house. There is a toilet for you to relieve yourself, as well as a bathing tub where the water comes out of a spigot and a wonderful invention called a shower. It is a special room built off the bathroom where the walls are lined in marble, and several spigots spray water upon your body as you stand in it. There is even a machine that plays music while you cleanse yourself. I have spent many delightful hours within this chamber, enjoying the spray of hot water hitting my body and rejuvenating my spirit. I will take you there and allow you to enjoy the sensation while I lay out your clothing for the day. Once you are finished, we will get something to eat and compose our advertisements. Then we will take them down to the office of the newspaper. We will use a cab, as I have yet to learn how to drive one of the vehicles these people use for transportation."

Ian understood little of what Keith was telling him. The need for relief overrode anything else that assaulted his mind. Ahead of him, Keith opened the door to a room that surpassed any expectations Ian had just heard about the room meant for bodily needs. It certainly wasn't anything like the privies or garden robes he had visited during his lifetime. Instead of the foul smell from human waste being collected in one spot, the room smelled even better than his bedchamber or the sitting room where he had found Keith relaxing earlier.

He inhaled deeply and was surprised to smell something that reminded him of spring flowers.

"The scent you detect is from something called an air freshener," Keith said. "It is certainly more pleasant than the privy that I have used in the past. I must admit, I have become accustomed to these luxuries in a relatively short time."

Ian agreed. He, too, could easily become accustomed to such conveniences. The room itself was a wonder. In a secluded corner Ian found the large porcelain fixture that Keith referred to as the toilet. At Keith's instruction, Ian stood in front of it and allowed the urine to flow from his cock. With that pressure relieved, he realized that he needed to relieve his bowels as well. As though Keith had read his mind, he put down a ring and instructed Ian to sit down as though he were using the hole in the privy. When he finished, Keith showed him a roll of paper hanging on the wall.

"This is called toilet paper. It is used to cleanse your ass after you have relieved yourself. They think of everything in this modern society."

With the necessities finished, Ian looked around the room. A large glassed-in enclosure had to be what Keith called the shower. The walls were lined with marble and there were many spigots in various positions on each end of the structure.

"I will adjust the temperature of this for you, so you must watch to see how it's done. Any of these spigots could easily wash your body, but when all of them are employed, it is a relaxing experience. The large one with the round head is like a rain shower on a summer afternoon. I enjoy using it for rinsing the soap from my hair."

When the water was the temperature that Keith desired, he handed Ian a strange looking ball along with a bottle with a strange shape. "This is what you wash yourself with," Keith said, pointing to the ball. "The bottle contains body wash. I am certain you will find the scent of it more pleasing than the lye soap we were used to using when we lived in our own time."

Shari Dare

Keith flipped open the cap of the body wash and instructed Ian to sniff the contents. The smell transported him to the meadows of McGowan Manor after a spring rain.

"On the shelf, in the shower, is a bottle of shampoo for washing your hair and another that contains conditioner," Keith instructed.

"I understand shampoo being soap to wash your hair, although I don't understand why I can't just use this soap." Ian held out the bottle of body wash. "What is this conditioner of which you speak?"

"They have an invention called television. It brings pictures into your home. You will find it's a way to learn what many of the things in this time period are called. They have commercials, and according to them, conditioner keeps your hair healthy. From the look of that red mop of yours, you could use it."

Ian ran his fingers through his long hair and then over the stubble on his chin. "I can understand, even to me my hair feels dirty. If I were at home, I would insist the barber wash it for me before he cut it and before he shaved me. Of course, once I went in search of Tabitha, I learned how to shave myself as though I were any common man on the street."

"Things are different here. Once you finish your shower and get dressed, I will introduce you to the electric razor. Here, men do not go to the barber for a shave, nor do they visit him for the washing or cutting of their hair. They wash their own hair, shave their own beards, and go to the salon for haircuts. I went to one right after I arrived and found it wonderful to have a young woman cut my hair."

"How did you learn all of this?"

"Tabitha has many contacts in this century. There was a man here to meet me who had come forward before. She said that he also met Gwain but had no memory of it since this is something that is best not to tell many people. Here, they do not accept time travel. For some reason, this man is under Tabitha's control and once he has finished meeting the newcomers, she erases his memory of the event. I do not understand it, but there is much I do not understand in this or any other world."

Keith left the bathroom to give Ian privacy in the shower. When he opened the glass door, the steam of the hot water was refreshing. Above his head was a button and when he pushed it, music filled the enclosure. The sound was as pleasing as the lather that came from the bottle of body

34

wash he'd poured on himself. The scent that had been so pleasing engulfed his body and washed away more than just dirt. It took away the tension that was usually his companion. It was certainly more pleasurable than a bath that went cold and forced him to get out before he was completely relaxed.

After rinsing the lather from his body, he reached for the shampoo. That, too, had a pleasing scent and produced as rich a lather as the body wash. When he finished, he stood directly under the large round spigot and let the water run over the long strands of his hair. Once the shampoo had been rinsed, he took the bottle of conditioner from the shelf and poured a small amount into his hand. It was much thicker than the shampoo or the body wash. After putting it on his hair, he marveled at how smooth his tangled locks felt.

When he finished his shower and head wash, he grabbed two of the large drying clothes. One he used on his body and the other on his hair. After drying himself, he wrapped the first cloth around his waist and the other he hung over the door of the shower.

On the counter, under the large wall of mirrors, he found a comb and ran it through his hair. It surprised him that there were none of the tangles that he usually encountered after a good night's sleep.

"You look refreshed," Keith greeted him. "I've laid out your clothes for the day on the bed. You will find the fashions here to be quite different."

Ian completely understood what Keith meant. He was dressed in blue pants that looked as unfamiliar as the shirt which was made of a finely knit fabric. On his feet were low-cut boots that were made of white cloth of some kind. He followed Keith into the bedroom and saw clothing similar to those his new friend wore spread out on the bed, which had somehow been made. He wondered if a servant had come in while he was cleansing his body.

"I made your bed for you," Keith said, as though he had read Ian's mind. "You will learn how to do this for yourself. There are no servants in this condo. The only ones I have found are those who keep up the grounds. I have learned that people judge you here by the way your home looks. I have learned to clean and even cook when necessary.

Shari Dare

There is no woman in this time who would consider being with you if you cannot keep your home presentable."

"This will be a bigger adjustment that I thought it would be. I've always had servants to do such things for me. I'm certain all of that will come to me, but for now, tell me how I should wear these clothes you have put on the bed?"

"Men in this time do not wear hose as we did. They wear underwear. There are many styles, but because of your age I chose a pair from the dresser that fit your body tightly. I think you will like the feel of them. I, on the other hand, like the looser cut, which are called boxers. Next, you will be wearing a pair of jeans. They are very comfortable, but also very different from what you are used to wearing. Instead of long hose, you will wear socks, and instead of boots, athletic shoes. As far as a shirt, you have your choice of a button-down shirt or what they call a polo shirt. Since the day promises to be warm, I think you would be happier with the polo shirt, like mine."

"You seem to know a lot about this time. How could you have learned so much in such a short period?"

"My guide was very informative and I have always had a mind for remembering things."

Ian put on the clothing, as Keith had instructed, and struggled with the closure of the jeans. He had expected hooks like what he was used to, but instead there was a metal button on the top and a strange thing that Keith called a zipper that held them closed so they could contain his unruly cock.

When he finished dressing, he looked at himself in the mirror over the dresser. The image that he saw was amazing. It certainly didn't look like the man he had been all his life. As he stared into the glass, his stomach began to rumble. He had thought little of his hunger until now.

"It sounds as though you are as hungry as I am," Keith commented. "Now that you are presentable, we will go out to the restaurant down the street and get something to eat. I think you will be pleasantly surprised by the selection they have to offer. It is far different from the food you are accustomed to eating at the tavern."

Ian followed Keith through the condo and out onto the street that ran in front of the building. The fresh scent of spring wafted through the air and filled Ian's lungs with the promise of a new life. Vehicles that were strange to him rushed past him at breakneck speed, without a proper horse and carriage in sight. Even the first impression that he had about the scent of the air was now ruined by the smell of what Keith called the exhaust coming from the vehicles. Even the smell of horseshit would have been more pleasing than this exhaust.

"These vehicles are called cars, trucks, and busses," Keith informed him, as he pointed at the vehicles. "The smaller ones are cars, the busses are used by people who want the privilege of being driven, rather than driving themselves to their destination, and the trucks are used for hauling goods, much like the wagons in our time.

The names of the vehicles rang bells in his memory. They were the names he'd been told of in the dreams that Tabitha had placed in the confines of his mind. Although they were strange, that wasn't what was frightening. It was the speed at which they traveled that caused his heart to race and fear to fill his mind.

Keith led the way as they walked down the street to the shop that he called a restaurant. The word was familiar from the dreams, but nothing Tabitha had planted could begin to describe the room into which they entered. A young woman greeted them and led them to a table that was set with a pristine white cloth and table silver, as well as napkins made from paper—at least that was what Keith called them.

Another young woman brought them a large book and invited them to look through the menu. The amount of delectable dishes that were listed made his mouth water.

"Since it is lunch time, I would recommend the soup and sandwich," Keith said. "I enjoy the one they call the hamburger. I order it with 'the works' as well as French fries."

Ian didn't argue. This was so new to him, he decided it was best if he order what had been suggested. He was pleased with the small cup of soup the woman called chicken noodle, but the sandwich and potatoes were delicious beyond compare. It was certainly different from the food that was served in the best houses of Inverness. There were no trenchers, nor did people sit at a high table. Here, it seemed, everyone was equal.

Once they finished eating, the girl returned to ask if they wanted what she called dessert. Keith nodded and ordered something he called "apple pie 'a la mode." "I tell you, you will think this is food meant for a God, especially when you taste the ice cream I ordered to put on top of it. While we wait for it to come, I think it is time for us to compose our advertisements for the paper."

They put the words down on paper, but it seemed as though Keith had something else on his mind. "Is something bothering you?" Ian asked.

Keith nodded. "Before I gave up my life to search for my nephew, there was a special lady in my life. I made certain she was well provided for, but I do wonder what has become of her. I doubt that you have heard of her, but I must ask if only to ease my mind. Have you ever heard of a woman by the name of Athena?"

Ian thought for a moment. How would he be able to tell Keith that the woman he mentioned was one of the best-known prostitutes in Scotland? It was said that she had been the mistress of an older man who had left her well-situated when he disappeared suddenly.

"I know of her. Her name is well known among the men of every major city in Scotland. Before I went to Inverness, Angus McGowan insisted that I enlist her services. It cost him a king's ransom for me to study with her for three months. Because of her, I was able to service the young wives of the elite of Inverness."

Keith smiled broadly. "You had a good teacher. Did she ever tell you about her life in the harem?"

"It was unbelievable at first, but she assured me that every word was true. I didn't know who the man was that saved her from such a life for she never named him. I should have known she had some connection to Gwain. Even Gwain's son visited her whenever he came to Inverness on business or just to see me. He spoke highly of the nights he spent, not only in her bed but also with the young women she trained in the art of sexual pleasures."

Keith nodded. "I am pleased that she had a good life and was able to make a living with the skills she learned as a young woman."

They left the restaurant and Keith flagged down one of the cars that sped down the road in front of the building. After stopping at the newspaper office to drop off their advertisement, Keith insisted they visit the beauty shop in the mall.

"I know that you said men didn't go to barbers in this time, but what is this beauty shop that you refer to?"

"There is much for you to learn, Ian," Keith said to set aside Ian's questions. "The barber shop is becoming a thing of the past. I learned that it is a pleasure to have a woman cut and wash my hair. From the people you have seen today, you must realize that the style of your hair needs to be modernized."

Ian agreed. He had seen many men in the restaurant as well as on the street and none of them wore their hair pulled back and tied with a ribbon the way he wore his. It was only fitting for him to become one with the times in which he now found himself living.

"You have beautiful hair," the woman who stood behind the chair said. She was facing the mirror in front of Ian. "Have you thought of donating it to Locks of Love?"

The only thing he understood about her question was *donating*. "What is this 'locks of love' you speak of?"

"There are children who are very sick and because of it the medicine they are taking causes them to lose their hair. With the length of your hair, it would be a wonderful donation in order to help them have wigs to wear."

Ian looked at the length of his hair and imagined it gracing the head of a sick child. The thought brought tears to his eyes. What kind of world had he come into that children were given medicine that made their hair fall out? He couldn't imagine such a terrible thing. Even if the treatment saved their lives, the thought of something making them even sicker than they already were upset him. In his time, children were a gift. When they became ill and died, it was God's will. How could these people be so selfish as to treat the illness and prolong the life that God wished to take for his own?

"Yes, I would like to do as you have suggested. It is unimaginable that something as simple as my hair could help a child, but if that be the case, I would be honored to participate in such a program."

The woman smiled, then turned his chair around and reclined the backrest. When she did, he found his head resting on the bowl of what must be a sink, for she began washing his hair with a scented shampoo that reminded him of the one he had found in his shower. After lathering his hair twice and rinsing out the residue, she added a conditioner. When she was finally finished, she raised the back of the chair and turned him again toward the mirror.

Even wet, his red hair glistened in the artificial light of the shop. He watched as she combed out any snarls that had formed since his morning shower, and then secured the wet strands with a band.

"This will make a lovely wig for a sick child," she said. She took the bound hair in one hand, and using the scissors, cut the hair just above the binding.

Ian swallowed hard, thinking of how long he'd been growing his hair and how much the women he'd bedded enjoyed running their fingers through his long locks. He prayed that the women of this time would be receptive to his new look.

A half hour later, Ian marveled at the change in his appearance. With his hair cut into a modern style, he resembled the other men of this era.

"You look much better," Keith said when he joined him at the receptionist's desk to pay the bill. "It is customary to give the young lady a tip for her services," he whispered.

Ian pulled out the plastic card that Keith had told him was acceptable for paying his bills and handed it to the young lady. As he had at the restaurant, he added a generous tip to the total before signing the receipt.

"Thank you, Mr. Brice," the girl said. "I hope when you come back you'll ask for me. Just remember, my name is Carolyn."

Ian knew he would be asking for this particular young lady in the future. If he were more comfortable in this new world, he would have asked her to share his bed. That would have to wait until another time, as Keith had reminded him that the women he should be courting were much older than this slip of a girl.

Chapter Five

"I've had it! I've just had it!" Emily Cranston said as she threw the new erotic romance she'd just bought across the room.

"Had it with what?" her friend and roommate Julie Langdon asked.

"Sex, that's what. If you believe what you read in these books, everyone's getting laid but me."

"At our age we can't expect miracles. I mean, I was never completely comfortable when Jack made love to me. I'm just as well shed of him. If you ask me, he's not the big time lover he makes himself out to be. Since we divorced, he's been through three more wives. It has to tell you something. Sex with him wasn't making love; it was being fucked, pure and simple. Once he got his jollies, to hell with me."

Emily sighed. She'd heard all about how Jack saw making love as a chore. If anyone was asexual, it was Jack. She should know all about him. She and Julie had shared the same house ever since the death of Emily's husband, Larry, five years ago. At the time she was struggling to make ends meet, and Julie had decided to sell her house and get out from under. It was the perfect situation for both of them. While Julie enjoyed cleaning the house and cooking, Emily reveled in keeping a garden and working outside. Their arrangement was a good one.

"Not everyone is getting laid, you know," Julie continued. "Most of our friends are happy with their grandchildren and their knitting."

"Well, I'm not. Even Maude Preston is dating and she's very verbal about her sexual experiences. Trust me, if I could get half the action that old heifer is getting, I'd be happy."

Julie laughed at Emily's statement. "What about Bill Watson?"

"What about him?"

"He seems to keep you busy and he talks a good show when it comes to sex."

"That's all there is, a lot of talk. When it's time for action, we either have to wait for the Viagra to work, if it works at all, or revert to using the pump. That's about as exciting as watching grass grow. Of course, that's only the foreplay. He can't do it in a normal position. His acid reflux is so bad, I have to put my legs over his shoulders and that kills any sensation for me. The only thing I can think about is the arthritis pain in my legs. Talk about being fucked. That's just what it's like. I haven't had a decent orgasm since Larry died."

Julie was laughing so hard she could barely talk. "So, what do you plan to do about it?" she finally asked.

"I picked up one of those free papers in the grocery store and read the personal ads. Some of those guys sound pretty damn good."

Across the room Julie rolled her eyes. "You can't be serious."

"Oh yes I can. I've got a couple of them marked. There's one for you and one for me."

"Leave me out of this. I don't want to be part of your fantasy."

"No way. They always say there's safety in numbers. Besides, this guy is perfect for you. Listen to this. '*Older white gentleman looking for an older woman for dinner, dancing, movies, plays and companionship*'."

Julie smiled, apparently intrigued by the image the ad provoked. "He does sound promising. Who did you find for yourself?"

"This guy stood out from all the others. '*Single white male looking for a meaningful relationship including sex with a mature woman*'. The ad says he's in his thirties."

"Good God, he's younger than your kids. I hope you know what you're getting into."

"Me too. I'm planning to answer both these ads through the e-mail address. I can set up blind dates for both of us and take it from there. Who knows, we could both get lucky."

Emily knew Julie was appalled by the fact that she was planning to actually answer the ad and set up the date, but it didn't matter. Since they'd agreed to share expenses, they shared everything else in their lives. "If worse comes to worst, we can walk out together. Besides, neither of these guys knows how to find us since the way I planned it, we'll be meeting them at the restaurant. If we don't feel comfortable with either of them, we can go to the ladies' room and get out of there."

"It sounds like you've got all the bases covered, but this blind date thing has me spooked. I realize we can leave and they can't find us, but how do we know they aren't ax murderers or serial killers? You know what they say about them. You never suspect until it's too late."

"You watch way too much *Tru TV*. Not everyone who puts an ad in the 'lonely heart's' column is a cold-blooded killer out looking for his next victim. If nothing else, we'll have a good time and a free meal at a great restaurant. If I get this sent out right away, I should get confirmation through my e-mail this afternoon. I suggested going to the Stagecoach. If they go along with it, we have some major shopping to do. With any luck, they'll want to meet us for dinner tonight."

"T-tonight…That's pretty sudden, isn't it?"

"If we're going to jump into this, I didn't want to give you any time to back out on me. Since it's already noon, we have to rush to be beautiful by seven when we go out to the Stagecoach to meet our dates!"

Julie rolled her eyes but Emily ignored the gesture. Instead of saying anything, she grabbed her purse and handed Julie her bag as well. They had a lot of shopping to do, including a stop at the beauty shop for complete makeovers.

By the time they got home, Emily's e-mail contained a confirmation of their date for seven at the Stagecoach. She was glad she had insisted that they go to the beauty shop and get new outfits. As it was, they had only three hours to get changed and drive out to the restaurant.

* * * *

"We received an answer to our advertisements," Keith said as he entered Ian's condo without knocking.

"So soon? We only placed them yesterday."

"That's right, but the paper came out this morning and apparently there are two women interested in meeting us for dinner tonight at the Stagecoach."

"The what?"

"The Stagecoach. It's a restaurant outside of town. We can have a cab take us there. Hopefully, the ladies will gladly give us a ride back here. Yours is named Emily and mine is Julie. I hope you haven't bitten off more than you can chew."

Ian studied Keith's face and saw the mischief in the older man's eyes. "Just what are you talking about?"

"I'm only saying that this Emily you will be meeting is not a starry eyed young woman who is anxious to know how to please her older husband. For this one a rich man who wants an heir won't pay you."

"And just what kind of woman do you think I will be bedding?"

"From what I have learned, the women of this day and age are well-versed in the activities of the bedroom. There are some who expect much from their lovers. I have heard great things about you, but are you up to bedding an older woman with great expectations of your prowess?"

Ian laughed. It mattered not if the woman was a virgin or a seasoned lover; he had never met his match. He certainly wouldn't do so tonight. If he were in luck, the woman named Emily would grace his bed tonight and if she pleased him, maybe for many nights to come. It could be that she would lead him to Gwain faster than he could find the man on his own.

* * * *

Ian found that the restaurant the women had chosen was indeed more like an inn in the country, like the one Keith had taken him to the night before. Fields flanked the building to the south and east, with paved roads on the north and west. He recognized the crops that were growing as corn on one side and some sort of grain on the other. He couldn't tell if it was oats, wheat or barley, but at least he was able to identify the crops that grew in this part of the world, to say nothing of this time period.

He had been concerned about how they would know the women they were coming to meet, but as soon as he entered the rustic building, he saw them sitting at the bar. He found he felt more comfortable in this restaurant than he had in the more modern ones. It was easy to picture this place in the Scottish countryside where weary travelers came to rest from their journeys.

Ian followed Keith's lead and made his way to the bar where the women sat sipping drinks. That, he found, was one of the hardest things he had to accept in this new time and place. In his day, only coarse bar wenches were found drinking ale or even whiskey at the taverns that many men frequented. Cultured women sipped tea or on occasion sherry, in the drawing rooms of their elegant homes. Here women, both young and old, went to the taverns or bars, as Keith had corrected him, in order to meet eligible men or just to relax.

He assessed both women who sat at the bar. Both were slightly plump, as were most of the women their age in Inverness. The difference came not only in their dress, but also in the way they wore their hair. Where he would have expected long gray tresses that were worked into elaborate braids and piled upon their heads, both women wore their hair cut short, and the color did not belie their age as much as their mature appearance.

"I am Keith Fletcher," he said, and extended his hand to one of the women. "And this is my nephew, Ian Brice."

The brunette took Keith's hand in hers. "I'm Emily Cranston and this is Julie Langdon."

Ian studied both of the women. Emily's eyes sparkled with anticipation, while Julie looked relieved to see that Keith was going to be her companion for the evening. From the expression on Julie's face, it was evident that she was less than excited about the possibility of spending the evening with two strangers.

As much as Ian wanted a whiskey to calm his nerves, he saw that the women were drinking beer and followed their lead. He didn't want to dull his senses just in case he would be taking Emily to his bed this evening.

"Your table is ready," the man who Ian decided must be the innkeeper said, interrupting their conversation.

Ian held out his hand to Emily, inviting her to take his arm. He escorted her to the table as though she was one of the highborn women he was used to courting. Emily smiled at his outdated ways in comparison to the men he had observed at the restaurant last evening who led the way, expecting the women to follow like little lost sheep. The manners these men had were deplorable, making him wonder how they had been raised. It certainly wasn't with any of the social graces. Even in McGowan Manor, he had learned the proper way to be with a woman when he was courting her. Between Angus and Davida, he had learned the manners meant to impress even the most highborn of the women with whom he associated. Had that part of his training been left to Charles, he doubted he would have been in such great demand by the wealthy men of Inverness.

"How delightful it is to be escorted by a gentleman," Emily commented, as he held out her chair so that she could seat herself.

"I agree," Julie said. "You certainly have better manners than most of the men I know. Are things so much different in Scotland than they are here? If they are, I give my compliments to your parents."

"Speaking of parents, how could you leave your families to come here?" Emily asked.

Ian and Keith exchanged knowing glances. "Other than Keith, I have no family," Ian replied.

Emily's expression was one of sorrow. "Oh, how sad. I would hate to think that all of my family were dead and gone."

Ian knew he'd told no lies. With the amount of time he had traversed, there was no way that either of his brothers was still alive. Of course, if he looked hard enough, he was certain he could find descendants of his brother Kyle, even though he would never find any from Evan. If he dug far enough, he might even find heirs from the nights he spent in the arms of the elite of Inverness.

"My mother left when I was but a wee lad. As for my father, he died before I was old enough to make my own way in the world. I was raised by my uncle." He had told no lies. To him, his father had died the day he sent him to McGowan Manor. He knew the fact that Charles McGowan was his second cousin by marriage and not really his uncle didn't make any difference. It was something that could never be proven in this modern society.

"What about brothers and sisters?" Julie pressed.

"My older brother Kyle died young and my brother Evan joined the priesthood. Since I was never much of a churchgoer, I have not seen him since he left home. It is possible that he, too, has joined Kyle in his eternal rest." *Again, I told no lies. Kyle said that I was dead to him as soon as he learned that our mother was whoring herself with one of the crofters. From the manor, I was sent to the monastery to be raised by Evan and the other priests. It was said that once they learned the reason for him being sent away, even he turned his back on his bastard brother. To me, they were dead long before they actually passed over the barrier between life and death.*

"How kind of you to take Ian under your wing," Julie commented, putting her hand over Keith's.

The look in Keith's eyes told Ian that his so-called uncle had found romance, and he wondered how long it would take the older man to get Julie in his bed.

"It was not until Ian was old enough to seek me out that I even knew of him. He was raised in another household. I was pleased when he found me and made his presence known."

"So," Julie began, "why did the two of you decide to come to the United States?"

Ian relayed the story the two of them had concocted as to how they came to be in Minter, Wisconsin, rather than Scotland.

"Keith and I both wanted something different in our lives. Since Keith had decided that he no longer wanted to be a gentleman farmer, he sold his holdings. I followed suit and sold my wool business. We have come here looking for adventure."

Both of the women laughed at his statement. "I'd hardly call Minter a hot spot for adventure, but it depends on what one is looking for," Emily said.

Before either of them could comment on what she had said, the waitress brought a strange looking tower to their table. The metal structure had four round holders, each containing a bowl with a serving of what their companions referred to as salad. Ian tasted each of the offerings, which included beet salad, three bean salad, corn relish, and one made of a tart cabbage that Julie identified as sauerkraut. Ian had to admit that he liked the variety he found in these salads. He remembered the abundance of meat on the tables of the manors and homes in Scotland, but they could not compare to the lighter fare he found in the restaurants of the twenty-first century.

When the main course was brought, he marveled at the entrées each of them had chosen. Julie ordered shrimp scampi and Emily deep fried lobster, while Ian and Keith opted for steaks since there was no mutton on the menu.

"Have you ever tasted deep fried lobster?" Emily asked. Ian shook his head no, too awed by this delicacy to put voice to his answer. "Then you're in for a treat," she continued, taking the small fork and spearing one of the round balls. After dipping it in butter, she popped it into his mouth as though she was a mother introducing a new food to a small child.

Ian savored the taste of the lobster encased in the delicate batter, dripping with melted butter. It was indeed different from anything he'd ever eaten, but he still craved the steak he had ordered. Another time, when his sensitive palate was more accustomed to the delicacies that the restaurants in this new time offered, he might be tempted to order one of these strange sounding dishes.

Julie, too, insisted that Keith try her shrimp. From the look on his face, Ian could tell that his friend was also intrigued by the taste of this dish neither of them had heard of in the past.

Rather than the rich desserts that they had ordered over the past couple of days, Emily asked for an after dinner drink menu. The names of the drinks were intriguing. They ranged from Pink Squirrel, Brandy Alexander, and Grasshopper, to a more traditional Whiskey Neat.

Since their female companions opted for the Pink Squirrel and Grasshopper, Keith ordered a whiskey and Ian decided to try the Brandy Alexander. He knew that having whiskey could easily lead to a drunkenness that might impair his ability in the bedroom, should Emily decide to come to his condo once the date was finished.

"We haven't been in this country long enough to have obtained our driver's licenses, so I'm afraid we will have to depend on the two of you to take us back to the city," Keith said.

"That won't be a problem," Julie replied. "We didn't know what you might want to do after we left here, so we brought separate cars."

"Why would you think of such a thing?" Ian asked.

"Keith said that he didn't drive when he replied to the e-mail that Emily sent. I was hoping I could talk him into taking in a new movie at the mall after dinner. The late show doesn't start until ten."

The word "movie" brought to mind the picture that hung on the wall. When it was turned off, it was black but when Keith turned it on, pictures brought news and entertainment into the living room. He called it a *flat screen television,* and explained that news could be broadcasted from the farthest reaches of the globe and seen almost instantly in homes so that even the common folk thousands of miles away could know of these happenings instantly. As for the movies, they had watched several, as well as sitcoms and television dramas, with the hope of learning more about the lives they would be living until the time of their deaths.

Ian had to admit he did not enjoy the noise of the television as much as Keith did. Although the movies and other things they watched were intriguing, he especially enjoyed the solitude of losing himself in the pages of the many books that lined the walls of the building Keith called the library. Television for him was a diversion, but reading was a real pleasure.

"That leaves the two of us to our own devices," Emily said. "I would adore seeing where you live. Earlier, Keith mentioned that you own one of the condos on the north side of town. Would you be willing to show it to me?"

Emily's question intrigued Ian. He had hoped to bed her tonight, but her suggestion of seeing where he lived made it evident that she was as anxious to enjoy the bed sport he had to offer as he was to show her.

"I would be delighted to take you to my home. I find that the people in this country live in much more luxury than I am used to."

"How can you say such a thing?" Julie inquired. "Unless you have led us astray, you and Keith are wealthy men. I'm certain you don't live in a hovel."

Keith laughed loudly. "I lived in an old manor house that has been in my family for generations. No matter how much remodeling is done, it cannot compare to the new condo I have purchased here."

"It's the same with me. I lived in a small flat in Inverness. I required nothing more. It was Keith who found this place for me. I'm still getting used to all the modern conveniences that I didn't have in Scotland.

Truthfully, I usually live a very simple life. What you take as normal here is not as normal in other places in the world."

"I suppose you're right about that. I have a friend who lives in London. She only recently bought a modern condo. Prior to that she lived in a row house without central heat. When I visited her in the eighties, she had just gotten her first washer and was bragging about the refrigerator she had also just purchased. I didn't say anything, but my side by side would have easily accommodated both her stove and refrigerator. So I guess I know what you mean. I know she had plenty of money, but she still shopped at secondhand clothing stores as well as secondhand furniture stores. That could be why she had the money and I didn't. I like to spend too much."

Emily's comment brought laughter from everyone at the table.

"I can vouch for Emily's spending habits," Julie said, "but then again, I never say no when she wants to go shopping. We both have the same talent when it comes to spending our money, sometimes foolishly."

Chapter Six

With dinner ended, Emily could feel her stomach begin to churn. Within a matter of moments, she would be driving toward town and an evening spent in Ian's condo. She wondered if he would want to go to bed with her tonight and if he would want to get to know her better. While she wanted to go to bed with him and share delightful sex, she also wanted to know more about him before jumping into something she might regret in the morning.

The way he talked about his home in Scotland struck her as odd. She also had friends in Scotland, and when they talked about their sons' flats in the major cities, they often mentioned how modern they were. From listening to Ian, it was as though television, as well as cars and many other things she took for granted, were completely foreign to him. Rather than coming from a different country, it was as if he came from a different time and place altogether.

The spring evening promised a beautiful day tomorrow, but for now Emily was more interested in the night that spread before her like the answer to her prayers.

"Would you like to drive?" she asked as they approached her car.

"I had better not. Keith has told me that we will be going to a driving school since things are so different here than in Scotland. Once I get my license, I will be more than willing to take you anywhere your heart desires."

Emily nodded and got into the car. Before she started the engine, she buckled her seat belt and watched as Ian did the same. Throughout the evening, she had gotten a good idea of where Ian and Keith lived.

"Keith's condo is the one on the end and mine is next door. Keith has decided that I should hire a housekeeper since he says my cleaning leaves a lot to be desired."

"Julie says the only reason we get along so well is that she enjoys doing the housework and I'd rather be working in the yard or the garden. I'm the first to admit that I'm not the world's best housekeeper. A little clutter never hurt anyone, in my book."

Ian chuckled. "It sounds like we'll get along just fine. Hopefully, you will be able to help me find a housekeeper that I can employ. I would ask Julia, but I have a feeling she will be preoccupied with Keith. I certainly hope so, because that would get him out of my hair."

After parking in front of Ian's garage, she put her hand on the door handle. When Emily felt the cold metal beneath her fingers, she withdrew it as though she'd touched a hot burner on the stove. She remembered how he had held open the door for her at the restaurant. At the time, he told her that a proper lady should never open a door for herself when there was a man to do it for her. The only man in her life who had insisted on opening doors for her was her father. Only in her wildest imagination could she equate Ian with her father in any way than this.

Her internal musings were quieted when Ian opened her door and held out his hand to help her out of the car. After locking the doors behind her, she allowed him to take her arm and escort her to the front door of his home.

She'd been curious about these condos but had never seen the inside of one of them before. The foyer had a high ceiling with a suspended light fixture, with panels that acted as prisms casting light about the room. The living room was furnished in a masculine fashion and the kitchen was one of the most modern ones she'd ever seen. Marble counters and the smooth cooktop stove accented the stainless appliances. She was anxious to see the bedroom. He had advertised that he was interested in sex, hopefully as much as she was, so this would be the most important room in the house.

She gasped in delight at the size of the room. Along with the king-sized bed, massive chest of drawers, and mirrored dresser, there was a sitting area with a chaise lounge, a matching chair, and a small table in between them.

"I never expected to see anything like this in one of the new condos. So often new construction gives you much smaller rooms."

"I was impressed when I first saw it myself. The rooms in my flat in Inverness were nowhere near this large. I think Keith did a good job in choosing these accommodations on my behalf."

"Why was it that he came here before you?"

Ian stood quietly for a moment, as though trying to formulate an answer to her question. "He made the decision to relocate here before I did. Once he was here, I decided to follow him. It was only natural for him to help me out by finding this place close to his. It is comforting to have him so close at hand when I need help understanding the ways of this country."

Some of Emily's qualms were quieted by his explanation. The reason he left Scotland had nothing to do with the male magnetism that seemed to emanate from him and was driving her crazy with desire.

The bed, which dominated the center of the room, had a magnetic pull for her, but instead of leading Emily to it, Ian guided her toward the chaise. At first glance, she thought it too small for two people, but as soon as she sat down, she realized there was enough space for both of them to occupy it together. She smiled at the fact there was enough room for both of them to recline against the backrest comfortably.

He put his arm around her shoulder and pulled her closer to him. Excitement ran through her body and made her tremble.

"Is something wrong?" he asked.

Unable to put voice to the fears that he was stalling rather than making love to her, Emily remained silent.

"I am afraid you are worried about making love to a complete stranger. These things cannot be rushed. We will make love, but not until both of us are ready for this. I am adept at loving women, but not before they are completely relaxed and ready to receive me as their lover."

Without further conversation, he covered her mouth with his. In the past she'd been kissed, but never before had she been kissed like this. His tongue traced around the rim of her lips as though begging for her to part them to allow him entrance. When she did allow him to slip his tongue between her parted lips, she felt sensations she'd never felt in the past. She and her husband had once tried to French kiss, but neither of them had been adept at it. At the time she decided she didn't like it and never tried to do it again. None of her other lovers had ever tried it, leaving her unprepared for the sexual sensations that a proper French kiss shot through her body.

As much as she wanted to jump his bones, she refrained. He had said that these things couldn't be rushed and she agreed with him.

As his kisses became deeper, he worked the buttons on her blouse. She would have sworn he never saw a bra before from the way he stared at her bra-encased breasts. Apparently, women's apparel in Scotland was different from what she wore. Rather than embarrass him, she leaned forward and unhooked the clasp, freeing her breasts for his inspection.

She held her breath as he looked at her less-than-perfect breasts. Of course, what could you expect of a body that was sixty-something? They certainly weren't as perky as they had once been, especially since the intervention of gravity that made them droop rather than stand up. At least she could cover them with a bra and give people the idea that nothing had changed in that area.

"You have a beautiful body."

Emily tried to hide the smile that tempted to cross her lips. "Thank you, but I'm no longer a young woman. I try to tell myself that I'm still sexually attractive to a man, but..."

"But nothing, my dear Emily. Beauty is in the eye of the beholder, and I find your beauty equal to any woman I have seen in many years. I want to make love to you, but I do not do so unthinking. I know the advertisement read that I was interested in sex, but after meeting you I am more interested in the woman than the act."

Emily could feel the blush that was creeping into her cheeks. It had been far too long since a man had told her that she interested him. Bill Watson certainly wasn't the lover she wanted in her life. She prayed that Ian was telling her the truth and not just leading her on.

* * * *

Ian watched the tears that formed in Emily's blue eyes. She was a beautiful woman. It was a shame that older men had no idea how to satisfy women their own age. He wondered if her experience with the older generation would have been the same if she were twenty years their junior. It was something he vowed to ask Keith about tomorrow. For now, he had a woman to romance. He hoped that she would enjoy the lovemaking that he planned for the remainder of the evening.

He took one of her ample breasts in his hand and manipulated her nipple until it pebbled under his expert touch. It was true; she was not the young, inexperienced woman he was used to being with. This was going to be an experience of a lifetime for him. In fact, he was certain there were many things he could learn from this woman.

He lowered his head to her breast and began to suckle. After sliding his hand down the elastic waistband of her skirt and her panties, he dipped his fingers deep within the valley that held the hidden cave of her cunt. Once inside her, he could feel the internal muscles contracting around his fingers. The thought of how it would feel to have those same muscles massaging his cock make him even harder than before.

Reluctantly, he allowed her nipple to slip from his lips. "I want to see you naked. There are too many clothes separating us. I want to glory in what makes you completely female."

She said nothing, but nodded her head in agreement. Before he could assist her in removing the remainder of her garments, she reached for his coat. Slipping it off his shoulders, she started to unbutton his shirt and then his pants. Her hands were everywhere, pleasuring him as much as he knew he had pleasured her over the past few minutes.

Emily ran her hands over the fur of the hair on his chest and flicked his hard male nipples with her manicured nail, causing him to gasp with pleasure. He certainly wasn't used to women who were this bold in their lovemaking. He'd considered himself an accomplished lover and always thought he got as good as he gave in sexual pleasures. He didn't know that the foreplay he so enjoyed with the women he bedded could be turned on him.

"What are you doing to me, woman?" he finally asked.

"Haven't you ever had a woman do this to you before?"

"I must have been with the wrong women. What you're doing is delightful torture. I'm almost afraid to ask what other tricks you know."

She purred at the acceptance of her abilities in the bedroom, and then slid his pants and briefs down off his hips. Once his cock burst free from the constricting underwear, Emily curled her fingers around his thick shaft and began to move the foreskin up and down.

"Now this is refreshing," she said, as she scrutinized his cock. "Most men are circumcised, but I see that you're not. My husband wasn't circumcised and I found him to be a better lover because of it."

Ian searched his mind. *Where have I heard the word "circumcised" before?* He pondered his silent question, and then remembered hearing the priest who came to McGowan Manor reading about such things. It seemed to have something to do with the Jews. *Does this woman think I'm a Jew? How can that be with my Scottish background? Just the thought of it would be enough to make the Holy Father blush.*

"I didn't want my son circumcised," Emily continued, "because I couldn't stand to have his wife not know the thrill of being with an uncircumcised man. Of course, I was overruled. The doctor said it was necessary for health reasons. I didn't agree, but I wasn't given a choice in the matter. I have to admit, his little penis was easier to clean, but at the same time I grieved over the fact that he would never be able to pleasure a woman in the way that his father could."

Ah, so that is it. The Jews in the Bible must have been far ahead of their time. I can understand why it would be easier to cleanse a baby who doesn't have a foreskin to contend with. There were times I wished I didn't have it, but I knew no difference. Now this woman is telling me that an uncircumcised man is a better lover. It makes me wonder how many lovers she has had in her life.

Ian ceased his mental ramblings when Emily began to move her hand up and down, making him harder than he could ever remember being in the past.

"You are killing me, woman. I need to be encased within the folds of your cunt and give you the same pleasure you have given me."

Without giving her a chance to protest, Ian swept Emily into his arms, picking her up from the chaise. He laid her down on the king-size bed and opened her legs to see not only her folds, but to enjoy the view of a more mature woman. He was used to the young wives of the elite of Inverness. With this woman, the tight curls of her mounds were replaced with longer, straighter hairs that were more sparse and tinted with the gray hairs of age. On further inspection, he noticed her clit and realized that it was larger than those young women. He had no problem finding it and massaging it until she screamed with the pleasure he was giving her.

"Now you are the one who is killing me. Fuck me, Ian, and give me the release that I know you crave."

Not heeding her request, he continued to give her pleasure until she came in his hand. Dipping his fingers into her, he felt the creamy cum that confirmed she was more than ready for him to enter her. As was his practice, he put his finger into his mouth and tasted the sweetness of her. It surprised him when he did. Her essence, tempered by age, was even sweeter than that of the younger women he had tasted in the past.

Just the taste of her tempted his cock and urged him to plunge himself deep within her velvety folds. As soon as he did, he realized that she was more than ready to accept him. Her internal muscles constricted around his cock, making him more excited than before. It was evident that age had given her more experience in how to pleasure a man.

Time and time again, he made her cum but withheld his climax so that she could have a more fulfilling experience. When he finally allowed his body the release it had been craving, he knew she had been well satisfied.

Basking in the afterglow of their lovemaking, he realized this woman was the perfect partner for him. Experience, it seemed, was worth far more in the bedroom than the youth of the women he'd been with in the past. Things would never be the same for him. In his time it would have been unthinkable to bed a woman of Emily's advanced age. In fact, he had never known any women who lived beyond the age of sixty. It was evident in this new time and place that women of sixty were not considered old, but in the prime of their lives.

Chapter Seven

Keith watched as Emily and Ian drove away from the restaurant. He was beginning to wonder what he had gotten himself into. With no idea of what to expect this evening, he worried that he might say the wrong thing and make Emily question his ignorance about going to what she called the 'movie theatre'. He certainly hoped it would be like watching television, but having read the caption that came with many of the movies he saw on television about it being adapted to the smaller screen, he knew the theatre must have a much larger viewing area.

"I do enjoy American movies," Keith commented, once Julie started the car and prepared to pull out of the parking lot. "It was something that I rarely saw when I lived in Scotland. I have to admit, since coming here I have become addicted to them. This will be the first time I have gone to a movie theatre though. I am looking forward to the experience. To see them on a large screen must be very different from enjoying them on television."

Julie smiled. "I can't believe that you've never been to the movies. It's one thing that I have enjoyed over the years. My former husband always told me that I was a fool to spend so much time and money on such a silly pastime."

At least she isn't married. Does she still grieve for her husband? "How long has your husband been dead?" Keith asked.

"Oh, he's not dead. We've been divorced for quite some time now."

"Divorced?" Keith questioned. The word wasn't one he'd been familiar with until he started watching *Divorce Court* on morning television. "Then that is why you are free to be out with me. What of

58

your husband? Has he remained in the area so that you can see him often?"

"Jack has been married three more times since our divorce. I guess I'm not the only one who thought he wasn't much of a lover. He moved out of state about two years ago. I say good riddance to bad rubbish."

"It is a shame that you have been so disappointed in love. My wife and I were married for many years. Even though I took a lover after her death, I still revered the years that the two of us spent together."

"You had a lover?"

"Yes, she was a lovely young woman. We became friends and then lovers. I allowed her to live in my home until I decided to move to this country. I made certain that she was well cared for when I left. I'm certain she was quite satisfied." *That's an understatement. According to Ian, Athena became a very successful woman after she left my home. It was only fitting that I gave her the means to support herself.*

Once back in town, Emily drove to the shopping center that wasn't far from the condo complex where Keith lived. At the end he saw the neon sign that read Movies 10. The building was huge but the parking lot didn't have many cars in it.

After she parked in the nearly empty lot, they went into the lobby of the theatre. Large posters depicted the movies that were playing. He left the choice up to Julie, who decided they should see an action movie called *Journey to the Center of the Earth*. It was surprising when she asked the person who sold them their tickets for the senior citizen discount.

It was true they were no longer youngsters, but it was amazing that the girl in the booth actually gave them a discount on the price of the ticket because they were older. For the first time, he found that being an older man had benefits.

* * * *

Julie hoped no one would ask her about the movie she'd just seen. If they did, she wouldn't know what to say. It was hard to concentrate on the movie with Keith so close to her, especially when he snaked his arm around her shoulder.

Sitting in the upper deck of the darkened theatre made her feel as though she was back in high school and on a date with one of the football players who was all hands when they went to the movie. Back then she would have slapped the boy's face, but tonight was different. Keith wasn't taking liberties but his intentions were obvious.

I'm not like Emily, am I? I can live without sex. At least I have lived that way since the divorce, as well as before, so why does this man make my panties wet just by putting his arm around me?

"It's been a long while since I've been with as delightful a wench as you," Keith said, as the last of the credits rolled across the screen.

"I find that hard to believe. What about the woman you said you took as a lover after your wife's death?"

"Athena was very young, and although she was well-versed in the art of lovemaking, she shared none of my other interests. I was never at ease discussing fine art or literature with her."

"Didn't the two of you watch movies on television?"

"My manor house was very remote. I never had a television installed there. We enjoyed more simple pleasures, such as riding horseback, taking long walks. As much as I enjoyed reading good literature and admiring fine art, these were things she didn't share with me."

His description of the life he led in Scotland confused Julie. It was inconceivable that anyone would not have television installed, especially in a remote area. As much as she enjoyed her books and going to the movies, she enjoyed watching television as well and couldn't imagine not having one at home.

"Would you like to come back to my place for coffee?" she asked.

"I would like that. It will be interesting to see where you and Emily live. Is it common for single women to live together and share expenses?"

"Not really, but Emily and I have been friends for a long time and we both needed each other. It's worked out quite well for both of us."

She drove back to the house, wondering if he would want to pressure her to go to bed with him. Even if he did, she didn't care. In the few hours that she'd been in Keith's company, she'd come to enjoy him more than she ever thought was possible.

Julie could hardly believe it when the clock struck midnight. "How could it have gotten so late?" Keith asked. "I really should call a cab and go home. Can I see you again?"

"I would like that. Do you have anything special in mind?"

"I've been hearing about a theatre in the city of Madison. The people on the morning news say that *Evita* is a wonderful play."

"Oh, it is. I saw the movie, but a friend of mine saw the original cast in London and has been raving about it for years. I've been wanting to go, but I don't like going out alone at night."

"Ah, dear lady, then it would be my pleasure to escort you, if you don't mind driving. I wrote down the phone number to get tickets, thinking it might be something I would enjoy seeing myself."

After calling the cab, Keith kissed her with an urgency that promised there would be more evenings like this in their future.

Chapter Eight

Emily woke, wrapped in a man's arms. For a moment, she mistakenly thought she would turn and see that it was Larry who held her close. The remnants of sleep left her mind, making her realize that a much younger man, with a rock hard body, held her in the way her husband had once done.

Memories of the lovemaking she'd enjoyed with Ian flooded her mind. When she'd answered the ad in the personals column, she'd never expected the man who advertised for an older woman to become a lover who would take her to the highest of heights in sexual satisfaction. Even if their affair ended with the dawning of this new day, she would be content. The sex that she'd enjoyed with Ian was even better than any she'd ever enjoyed with Larry.

"Good Morning, Emily," Ian said, as soon as he opened his eyes. "Last night was very interesting."

Those certainly weren't the words Emily wanted to hear. She wouldn't call what they'd shared last night *interesting*. "What do you mean by that?"

"I have never been with a woman who is older than me. Until I met you, I had never considered such a thing. The older women I have known I would not wish to take to my bed."

"I still don't understand. You advertised for an older woman for the purpose of sex. Why would you do that if you had no desire for someone my age?"

"I came to this country on a mission for my cousin William. He sent me in search of his birth father, Gwain. All I know about the man is that he came here in search of an older woman. I was hoping that by meeting a woman of her age, I would be able to find him easier. Little did I know that the first woman who answered my advertisement would become a willing sexual partner. Any illusions I had about bedding an older woman disappeared last night. You are one of the most exciting women I have ever been with. I was hesitant to wake today, for fear that it had all been a dream. I no longer care about the man I came here to find, only the woman who found me through the advertisement. Promise me that we will be together again and again in the future."

Emily's heart jumped for joy. The thought of being with this man for more than an evening brought to mind all the erotic forms of lovemaking they could engage in over the next weeks, months, or if she was lucky, even years.

"I promise, because you are an exciting lover. I only hope I will continue to prove enough of a woman to keep you happy."

His answer came as a sensual kiss combined with the act of flipping her onto her back so that he could make delightful morning love to her. Last night had been a leisurely affair, designed to give both of them the highest amount of pleasure and satisfaction. This morning, he loved her with an urgency that said he couldn't get enough of her. He pumped against her, the foreskin of his cock pleasuring her as much as the full length of him inside her.

As though she was still a much younger woman, she wound her legs around his waist, to allow him to push even further inside her body, and tantalize the opening to her now-barren womb. Every nerve in her body responded to him, making her aware that there were so many different ways to make love that the two of them could try, and she knew she would never tire of him.

* * * *

"Do I have to ask how your evening with Ian went?" Julie asked when Emily returned home later that morning.

"I doubt it."

Julie laughed out loud. "I do too. Your lips are so kiss-swollen, I wonder if you had time for anything else last night."

Emily put her hands to her lips and smiled. "I can't begin to tell you what all we had time for. He's very knowledgeable and not just about good literature and theatre. We made delightful love and he wants to see me again tonight. I haven't been this satisfied in a long time. How was your evening with Keith?"

"That man is a perfect gentleman. We came back here and talked most of the night away. He's even getting us tickets for the theatre tonight. You know I've been dying to see *Evita* in Madison and he said if I would drive, he'd pay for the gas and get the tickets. He's even making reservations for us at my favorite restaurant. We're leaving at three this afternoon."

"Did he suggest going to bed with you?" Emily asked. It amused her to see the blush that crept up from Julie's neck to the roots of her graying hair. That told Emily more than any answer her friend could have given her.

"We talked about it. He said that it had been a long time since he had bedded such a lovely wench as me. I love the way he sounds so old fashioned."

Julie's comment started Emily to thinking about some of the things Ian had said during their lovemaking. He had referred to the wenches he had known in the past. "Do you think it's possible that these guys are from Scotland, but maybe not from modern-day Scotland?"

"What are you talking about?"

"Well, you know, like in those books where people time travel."

Julie laughed at Emily's comment. "You know that's fiction. Things like that don't really happen. I think you've been reading too many of those Sandra Hill books that you like so much."

"Maybe I have, but you have to admit it's a romantic idea. Can you imagine coming forward or going backward in time in order to find true love?"

"Not really, but I did find out that Keith is looking for another nephew named Gwain. Have you ever heard of someone by that name in this town?"

Emily shook her head. "Ian asked me the same thing. He said that this man is the birth father of his cousin William. I wonder what makes him so important to these two people."

"I don't know, but if I had a cousin or niece who disappeared, I would be out there trying to find her. Maybe it's the same with these two guys. I'm willing to make a few calls to our friends in order to help them out."

"What if we find this guy and Ian and Keith decide that they don't want anything to do with us? What if that's the only reason they're dating us? I'm not sure I want to take such chances, now that I've found at least a little bit of happiness and sexual fulfillment."

"Aren't you being a bit too self-centered? If it was you looking for a relative, how would you feel if someone who could have helped you refused to do so just to keep you by their side?"

Emily hung her head. "I'd feel used. I'd think the guy was a real jerk and downright selfish. In other words, I get what you mean. I'll be willing to make some calls and see what I can find out, just not right now. Let's enjoy ourselves for awhile first. I just hope it doesn't turn out that Ian is more interested in this Gwain than he is in me."

* * * *

"You look like a well-satisfied tomcat," Keith said, when Ian joined him to go out for lunch.

"I am well satisfied. Being with Emily is an experience that I never thought I'd enjoy. The things that woman knows boggles my mind. I didn't know that women had such knowledge. I am anxious to be with her again. She has as much to teach me as I have to teach her."

"What about Gwain?"

"We will find him, but nothing says I cannot have the delights I so enjoy in the bargain. How about you? Did you make your way into Julie's bed?"

"I don't work as quickly as you do, my young friend. I am taking Julie out to dinner tonight and then to the theatre. I suggested the play that I've been hearing about on television. It's called *Evita,* and to my surprise she wants to see it. She says it's a rock opera. The opera part I understand, but not the other. It will be interesting to see what it's all about. Meeting her has made me anxious to learn how to drive one of the automobiles that we see on the streets. It is not proper for the lady to be responsible for driving the gentleman when they are out for the evening."

"I agree with you, Keith. I have decided I want to learn how to drive as well. I also want to learn how to use the computer. Emily has told me of the many wondrous things she has learned from what she calls 'surfing the web'. She also says she gets messages from her friends that she calls 'instant messages'. She says she can carry on a conversation by typing a message onto the screen. It is all very interesting. I have been checking in the book that is by the phone you introduced me to yesterday. I find there are schools not only for how to run the computer, but also how to drive a car. I hope you don't mind, but I have enrolled us in these classes. This morning they will be here at eleven for our first driving lesson, and next week we will begin classes to learn how to run the computer."

"It is no wonder that you were a successful businessman in Inverness. I had not thought of looking up such schools. I only hope you aren't trying to learn too much too quickly. We came to this time and place in search of Gwain. If we become too involved in learning to drive, use the computer, and make time for Julie and Emily, will we have time to search for him?"

"We will *make* time, and if what Emily has told me about the computer is true, we will be able to use it to our advantage. She says that it is possible to do a search called 'Google' and learn about anyone in the world. It could help us find Gwain."

"What do you plan to do when you find him? We both know that neither of us can go back to the life we had before Tabitha sent us to the future. Will you be content with a woman like Emily? She's much older than you. Do you think you can live the rest of your life without fathering children?"

Ian pondered his answer. In the past he had fathered many children, but he couldn't call them his own. They had other names and other fathers. "The name of Brice was carried on nicely by my brother. If what he told me was true, I have no claim to it for I was my mother's bastard, fathered by someone who my mother went to in an attempt to dishonor my father. I have no desire to bring children into this world without giving them a heritage that they could be proud of. Emily is a challenge and one that I'm willing to take on."

Chapter Nine

On her way over to Ian's condo, Emily stopped at the local erotic shop. The shelves were stocked with everything from vibrators to feathers and flavored motion lotions. Normally, she would have gravitated to the dildos, but with Ian as her lover she had no need of anything so artificial. His cock rivaled anything she had ever purchased in the past or hoped to purchase in the future.

She moved on from the dildos and vibrators and found the counter that was stocked with motion lotions. For herself, she chose chocolate covered cherry and for Ian, her choice was raspberry cordial.

Her next stop was the jars filled with the various feathers. Amidst the ones that were made of fake fur, there were goose and peacock feathers. With great care, she fingered all of them and picked out the most beautiful of the peacock feathers to take with her to Ian's tonight.

All the while she was in the shop, she thought of the conversation she had engaged in with Julie earlier that morning. If Ian was a time traveler, why had he come to this place? She'd done an Internet search for Gwain McGowan, but the only name that came anywhere close was the McGowan clan. It told of a man named Charles McGowan who lived in the fifteenth century as well as his son William. From there, it went on to lesser-known members of the clan, but there was no mention of Gwain.

Since she'd run out of time, she decided she'd do another search with a different search engine tomorrow. Tonight Ian was waiting for her and she hoped she would make their time together something he wouldn't soon forget. Once she satisfied her sexual needs, she would turn her attention to the question of where one Mr. Ian Brice really came from. She had no doubt that he was a Scotsman, but what she really wanted to know was what time period he came from.

* * * *

Ian stared into the flames from the gas fireplace. Keith had told him that to lay a fire, all he had to do was flip a switch. Like so many things he found in this new time period, the fake flames made things easier, but he missed the smell of wood smoke.

Last night Emily had suggested she grill him a steak and bake him a potato. After eating in the restaurants he'd been frequenting, he found he liked the thick steaks as well as the baked potatoes. He told her that if she would do the cooking, he would do the shopping. After their driving lesson, he and Keith had gone to the supermarket just blocks from their condos. There he'd found bags of greens like the ones they'd enjoyed in the restaurants. He also picked out two steaks that were cut to his specifications by the butcher. Keith added butter, sour cream, baking potatoes, and a chocolate and strawberry torte to the basket.

Ian wanted to go next door to the liquor store for a bottle of good whiskey, but Keith suggested a fine red wine. Since he'd paid the bill with the plastic card that Keith had given him when he first arrived, he had no idea how much the groceries and wine cost him.

Keith had left for his date with Julie almost as soon as they had returned home, giving Ian time to take two of the roses from the bouquet they'd purchased in the grocery store. Carefully, he'd stripped the petals from the stem before strewing them over the clean sheets he'd put on his bed after getting up that morning.

The doorbell rang, reminding him this was something else that he needed to get used to. Why couldn't people in this day and age knock the way he was used to? The infernal music that came from nowhere was enough to drive a sane man crazy.

Without giving into his frustrations, he went to answer the door. Seeing Emily standing on his doorstep drove all petty thoughts from his mind. Last night she had been tentative and perhaps more than a little apprehensive about what the evening would hold. Tonight, she looked as though she was eager to share a meal with him in prelude to an evening in his bed.

"Good evening, dear lady," he greeted her.

"I hope it will be," she replied. "I hope I made good choices when I went shopping this afternoon."

He eyed the pink plastic bag she carried suspiciously. "Shopping?"

"I went to a little store called 'Naughty But Nice'. They specialize in erotic sex toys. In the past I've gone there to buy vibrators shaped like…" She hesitated, as though she was almost ashamed of the words that refused to pass her lips.

"Shaped like a man? I've read of such things. Why would a beautiful woman like you buy something like that when there must be many men who want to be with you?"

Emily lowered her eyes away from his gaze. "The men I know are more interested in watching television than they are in sex. There must be something wrong with me because I don't think of myself as old. I feel like I'm still thirty-five and madly in love with making love."

"And what is so wrong with that? If the men who are your age are no longer interested in making you happy, then their loss is my gain. There is nothing wrong in taking a younger lover. I have acted in that capacity for more than one old man who either cannot satisfy his young wife or can no longer get a child on her to carry on his name."

As soon as the words passed his lips, he regretted them. Keith had warned him not to mention the past that, until he'd time traveled, had been his present. He understood Keith's concerns. How could he expect someone like Emily to understand what he'd experienced when he didn't understand it himself?

"You're going to think I've lost my mind," Emily began. "I mean, I know it only happens in books, but is it possible that you're a time traveler?"

Ian was so shocked by her question that it took him several moments before he could answer her. "How did you know?"

"It was only a guess. Maybe it was some of the things you've said, or maybe it was just wishful thinking. I've always been interested in such things. To be truthful, I'm excited about the idea of making love to a man that has come from either the past or the future. So which is it? Are you an old fashioned man, or do you find your new life archaic?"

"I'm afraid I am very old fashioned, and the wonders of this time and place are amazing to me. The best wonder of them all is you. In my time, women tolerate the lovemaking of their men. I have the reputation of being a great lover. I have been employed by the wealthiest of men in Inverness in order to teach their young wives about lovemaking and to give them the children their older husbands cannot."

"I'm not young, Ian, and I can't give you children."

"I understand that. You must let me finish. In my time, women of your age do not want sex any longer. They do whatever they can to avoid it. I am pleased that you embrace it. I also like your adventurous nature. I am sure that there are things I can teach you, as well as things you can teach me."

"I agree, but before we start any lessons, I must ask how it came to be that you found yourself transported to another place and time."

Ian hesitated for a moment, and then told her about William's desire to have his father know of him and how he had gone in search of Tabitha. He left out nothing, including the fact that Keith had come before him. "We are both searching for Gwain, but I doubt that we will find him. Instead, we have found exciting women who will make the transition into our new lives easier. Whether your friend knows it or not, she is keeping company with one of the great lovers of his time. He's not about to push her into something she doesn't want, but when she's ready for him to make love to her, she'll be in for a pleasant surprise."

Ian didn't know if the expression on Emily's face was one of shock, disbelief, or contentment with a lover who was almost six hundred years old. His body was only that of a man of thirty years, but in reality it had been eons since he'd been with a woman, and last night Emily had opened herself to his lovemaking. He was looking forward to everything she had to teach him about this new time and place in which he found himself.

* * * *

Emily didn't know if she should use her cell phone to warn Julie about the lover who was taking her out tonight, or if she should cook dinner and relish the dessert she had picked up at 'Naughty But Nice'.

It took only a moment for her to decide on the latter of the two ideas. "I don't know about you, but I much prefer to make love on a full stomach. Why don't you show me the way to the kitchen so that I can get started making those steaks you promised me?"

"I never learned to cook, but I think it is something that I should know in this strange time. Can I help you?"

Emily couldn't believe that his very asking to learn how to cook could sound like an erotic suggestion. After agreeing to teach him how to grill a steak and microwave a potato, she followed him out to the galley kitchen.

From the refrigerator, she took out the steaks and opened the butcher paper. She liked the idea that these were steaks he had ordered especially for tonight.

"I begin by rubbing the meat with a combination of seasonings," she said, as she mixed together salt, pepper, and garlic powder.

"Like this?" he asked, as he began to rub his hand over her sensitive breast. "I don't have any seasoning, but I think I have the technique down."

Emily leaned back against Ian's chest as his fingers found her tender nipples and manipulated them through the material of her blouse and bra. "Even though you wear less clothing than the women I'm accustomed to being with, I find there is still too much material between my fingers and your delicate breasts."

These were the words she had longed to hear. This younger man saw her as a desirable woman. It was so different from being with the men of her age. She couldn't make any of them understand that even if they could no longer get it up, the words of love and the touch of their fingers on her skin were all she cared about.

"The steaks," she said, breathless with the way he was bringing her to full arousal.

"They can wait. For now I am hungry for your body. If I do not feed this hunger, it is entirely possible that I will die of starvation."

Expertly, he turned her until she faced him. She could see the lust in his eyes. He wanted her as much as she wanted him. Overcome with the passion radiating from him, she started to unbutton his shirt and run her hands seductively over the mat of red hair on his chest. When her fingers found his male nipples, she felt them pebble beneath her touch.

"To hell with dinner," she gasped. "I want to make you the main course."

"No more than I want to do to you. We can feed our stomachs once we feed our souls."

Without further words, he scooped her into his arms and carried her toward the bedroom. The bag of delights she had picked up at the sex shop lay unopened in the living room. At this moment, she needed no sex toys other than the hardness of his cock penetrating her cunt and taking her to the heights of pleasure. If she thought she needed outside stimulus, she was mistaken. All she needed was Ian and the pleasure she found within the confines of his arms. This was what she had longed for. It didn't matter that he came from another time and place. He was here, within her reach, and ready to give her the ultimate pleasure that a man could give a woman.

* * * *

Ian wanted to explore the items in the bag that Emily brought to his home tonight, but he wanted her more. He would examine the sex toys of the future later.

Once she was on the bed, he unbuttoned her blouse and as he had in the past, he marveled at the beauty of her breasts encased in the lace of her bra. The fact that her bra was almost transparent made her nipples look like a tempting treat. He reached behind her and unhooked the fastener that held the bra in place, freeing her ample breasts so that he could take them in his hands. He smiled to see that her nipples hardened as soon as he touched them.

He took one of her nipples into his mouth and began to suckle. As he did, he slipped his hand past the elastic waistband of her slacks. Instead of the silken barrier he'd found the night before, his fingers felt the hair that guarded her womanly delights. Probing further, he moved them into the wetness of her and found her clit. Massaging it in the circles that he knew would give her the greatest pleasure, he listened to her as she moaned.

Inside his pants, he grew hard, but he'd never been a man to take his own pleasure and leave the woman wanting. He would wait as long as it took for him to be certain she was completely satisfied and ready for him to take her.

"Oh Ian, don't torture me so. I want you, all of you."

Those were the words he wanted to hear. Removing his hand, he helped her out of her slacks. Once Emily stood before him naked, she reached for him. While he still had trouble with the zipper of his pants, she didn't. She not only undid the button at the top but she also slid the zipper down. Like her, he hadn't worn the underwear that Keith had provided him. He didn't like the feel of it against his cock. Even the pants he wore were coarse in comparison to the fine wool of the pants and kilts that had embraced his body all of his life.

When he was naked, Emily crawled back onto the bed. This time, instead of lying on her back with her legs spread, she got up on her knees. "Take me from behind. I've been told that there is deeper penetration that way."

"Have you ever done it this way? Do you have any idea what you're asking for?"

"I've never had a partner who would accommodate me. I only know what I've read and what I've seen in videos. I want to know what it feels like to be fucked from behind, to have you take command of my body in the way that the cavemen took their women at the beginning of time."

Ian thought of the women he'd bedded. The only time he'd taken a woman from behind was when he had been angry with a prostitute who had called him a whore for taking money to impregnate the women of Inverness. He had taken her in the most degrading manner he could think of in order to punish her for the hateful words that had cut him to the quick. He immediately thought of the woman he'd bedded while waiting to be transported to this time. He'd taken her from behind, not as a punishment, but to heighten her pleasure.

"Don't you find this degrading?" he finally asked.

She laughed at his question. "I find it exciting. Are you going to accommodate me?"

His cock throbbed in anticipation of making love to her in the most satisfying way he'd ever done it in the past. "I am willing to do anything that gives you pleasure, but if at any time I hurt you, I will stop."

He got on the bed behind her and straddled her knees with his. When he was in position, he guided his cock into her cunt. Once firmly imbedded within her folds, he leaned across her back and grabbed her tits in his hands, working them as though he were milking a cow while moving within her. Her screams were of pleasure, not pain. He felt as though he had penetrated deeper than he ever had before. His balls slammed against her ass every time he plunged into her. Their climaxes came at the same time, sending his seed deep within her body. If she had been one of the aristocratic ladies he was paid to impregnate, she would surely have carried his child as soon as he finished.

When they were done, he rolled her onto her back and wished for the love clothes that he'd used over five hundred years ago. Keith told him that in this day and age, love clothes weren't a part of lovemaking.

"That was fabulous. It was everything I expected and ten times more. From what I have read, in your time it was acceptable for the man to cleanse the woman after lovemaking. I think it's time for me to do the same for you. I noticed the elaborate shower you have. It seems to me it's the perfect place for me to cleanse you."

She got up from the bed and he watched as his creamy white cum trickled down her inner thighs. He followed her, like a dog followed a bitch in heat, anticipating the pleasure of mating with her.

Inside the shower, she turned on all of the jets before lathering the washing ball with the soap that came in the bottle. She ran her hands over the entire length of his body. When he reached for her, she shook her head no.

"You have given me such great pleasure that if I died tomorrow, I would die happy. There are so many other positions and things I want to try, and I'm hoping that I can give you enough attention when we're finished so that you'll be willing to do the things I've only read about."

"You are a remarkable woman, Emily. In the past, there have been many women to feel my cock within their inner walls. None of them have been adventurous enough to want to explore anything other than the normal positions. I wondered what things would be like in the future. I am now more excited than before about what my life has in store for me."

Emily ran her hands over his body as she smiled at what he could only call excited anticipation. "There is so much that I want to try. At my age it's hard to find a partner who is willing to do them with you. You're the answer to my prayers."

"What about your husband?"

"Like I told you before, he's been gone for several years now and even when he was alive, he was never as interested in sex as I was. He certainly wasn't into trying new positions. He allowed me to perform oral sex on him, but he wouldn't do the same for me."

"Oral sex?"

A wicked smile crossed her lips. "When we finish our shower, I will show you and maybe you will understand what I want."

"You are a delight, but for now I am afraid that the hunger that claws at my belly far exceeds that of my cock. Perhaps this oral sex that you speak of will be best if enjoyed on a full stomach."

Ian looked intently into Emily's eyes. He didn't want to disappoint her, but he found it was always best to speak the truth when talking with women.

* * * *

Emily liked the way Ian spoke his mind. He was a man with appetites but they weren't just for sex. It was important that they have their dinner. She certainly didn't want him to expire from hunger before they had a chance to explore every one of her sexual fantasies.

Delightful ideas rushed through her mind as she ran her hands over the entire length of his body, paying special attention to his cock and balls. She knew that the evening she had planned would include sucking not only on his cock but also his balls once she covered them with chocolate covered cherry motion lotion. All the time the idea grew within her mind, she wondered what she would taste like to him once she was covered in the raspberry cordial lotion. Would he enjoy it? She hoped so.

While Emily prepared the potatoes for the microwave and finished seasoning the steaks, Ian asked numerous questions. His thirst for knowledge of this new time into which he had been brought was refreshing.

By the time dinner was on the table, Ian told her he was certain he would have no problem preparing their next meal himself. "It's one thing to be able to grill a steak and another to be an accomplished cook," Emily teased.

"I know, but I do think I could handle a steak and baked potatoes. This is certainly food fit for the gods."

His comment brought to mind thoughts of the meals she'd read about in the numerous historical novels she'd bought over the years. "What are you used to eating?"

"In the time where I came from, the daily fare would have been mutton stew at the local tavern. There were no fine restaurants in Inverness like the ones I have found here. When I was fostered at my cousin's manor, supper was an elaborate affair, because the women had to cook for the men of the clan who took meals in the main hall. We would dine on roast duckling, trout, and mutton. I never gave much thought to the preparation of those meals before."

"It must have been a gigantic job. Those women more than likely had little time for anything other than cooking."

"There were many women in the kitchen, so the work was shared. Then there were others who kept the manor clean, but there was not the luxury in which you live. The floors were covered in rushes and by spring they had to be taken outside and burned to rid them of the vermin who lived in them all winter."

Emily could feel her skin crawl at the description. "Why did you live in Inverness and not at the manor?"

"My cousin's husband died when I was but a lad. It was his uncle, a man named Angus, who took over my education. He told me that since I had no lands of my own, I should use my mind to make a living. It was Angus who set me up in business in Inverness as one of the top wool merchants in the city. I repaid him many times over. It was the best thing I could have done. Not only did I have a lucrative business during the day, but at night I was paid well to help the older men in the city with young wives. When those wives were afraid of sexual relations with their husbands, I taught them the beauty of the act. I also gave those men the sons and daughters who would not have been born of their loins."

Emily was shocked by Ian's admission. "In today's society, it would be a woman doing such things. They're called surrogate mothers. They carry the child for the family when the woman can't get pregnant. As for the other, we have women called sex therapists who bring new spark into dull marriages. I always thought I'd like to do something like that, but I didn't have enough personal knowledge. All that I know is what I read in books and watch in the porno videos I purchase over the Internet."

"Then I think there is no time like the present to put all those things you've only read about and watched into practice. Your adventurous nature is exciting."

* * * *

While Emily loaded the dishwasher, Ian cleaned the grill. He was amazed that he had so easily spoken of the life he'd lived in the past to Emily. Keith had cautioned him to be careful about telling people he came from the past, but somehow the words had slipped out. Instead of being horrified, she had shown genuine excitement. Tonight would be a most pleasurable night for both of them. He would be learning the tricks of this new time and place, and she would, he prayed, be satisfied by his antiquated lovemaking.

"I'm finished," Emily announced, as the sound of the dishwasher coming to life filled the room.

"So am I," Ian replied, wiping the last drop of water from the grates of the grill that were built into the stove. Once he replaced them, he watched while she went into the bathroom in order to prepare herself for the evening ahead of them.

Just watching her brought to mind the joy of sharing the shower with her earlier. She had told him she was sixty years old, but it was certainly hard to believe. While her body was fuller than a younger woman, her muscles were well toned and the way her ample curves aroused him was amazing. He had known only a few women of her advanced age in his time period. They were mostly widows who were content to sit by the fire and work on their knitting while their grandchildren played around their feet. Sexual activity was, more than likely, the last thing on their minds.

Things were so different with Emily. She never mentioned her grandchildren and he couldn't imagine her sitting by the fire with her knitting.

* * * *

"Are you ready for tonight?" Emily asked, as she picked up the bag from Naughty But Nice. Just the thought of the delights hidden inside the pink plastic bag brought a smile to her lips. She could almost taste the chocolate covered cherry motion lotion she'd purchased. That, combined with the natural flavor of Ian's skin, was enough to make her panties wet in anticipation.

Earlier, their lovemaking had been for her gratification. Now she planned to play out a fantasy that had been with her for many years.

After donning the harem costume, along with the slave collar she had purchased in the sex shop, she came out of the bathroom. "I am here as your sex slave, Ian. My desire is to do whatever I can to make you happy."

Ian smiled wickedly. "You would do anything?"

"Within reason. I don't do anal sex, but I'm game for anything else. Of course, I have something in mind before you make any suggestions."

"Whatever it is you have in mind, I feel that perhaps we should go into the bedroom. I do enjoy being comfortable when my slaves do whatever they can to make me happy."

She wondered if she had made the right choice with the harem costume. "In your time, did you have slaves?" she asked timidly.

"I am told that the lover Keith had for so many years had, at one time, been a sex slave in a rich man's harem. He was on business in that area when she went up for auction and he bought her in order to give her the freedom she deserved. In return, she graced not only his bed but also that of Gwain. It was years later when I found her. She ran a house where men could go to be trained in the fine art of giving pleasure to women. My mentor, Angus, paid a high price for her services and they were worth the money that changed hands. If anyone was the slave it was me. After being with Athena, I was a slave to my sexual appetites and the purses of the older gentlemen of Inverness. They paid me well to show their young wives how to make love to them and to plant babies in their bellies."

"You were hardly a slave. It is more like you were a surrogate father. Did you ever get to see your children?"

"I never had a desire to see them. I did know when my sons were born, but I had no reason to want sons of my own. I did not learn until I was an adult the reason my father fostered me out at such a young age. My brother told me that my mother had been with one of the men in the village before I was born and my father never believed that I was his son. He sent me away in disgrace to be fostered by his cousin's husband. It wasn't a happy household and I vowed that I would never bring children into the world unless they would be loved and cherished. Every child that I fathered was done so to give a young woman pleasure and an old man pride. It wouldn't do for me to come back to claim them as my own months or even years after their birth."

Emily wiped the tears from her eyes. Ian was a giving man and he would have made a great father, but instead he gave life to children so that they could enjoy the life he had been denied.

Without making further comment, Emily followed Ian into the bedroom. Once there, she unbuttoned his shirt and helped him take it off. When she finished she ran her hands over the fine mat of red hair sprinkled on his muscular chest and teased his male nipples as she had done earlier.

He reached for her, but she shook her head no. "You are the master and I am the slave. I am to do for you and you are to enjoy what I do to you."

She reached for the button on his pants to undo before sliding the zipper down in order to release his cock for her inspection. From the bag she brought from the sex toy store, she took out the motion lotion and rubbed it generously on him. As she did, he grew larger than he had been when he took her from behind earlier. Before she started to give him a blow job, she pulled out the small whip she had also purchased.

"What is all of this?" Ian asked.

"These are sex aids. Things that make men and women enjoy sex with each other more fully. Since I am to be your slave, I bought a little

79

whip. I've read that some men and women are sexually turned on by spankings and whippings. I thought it was something we might try."

Ian pulled her into a tight embrace. "I need no toys to get sexual satisfaction. Is all that you know about what transpires between a man and a woman from books?"

Emily blushed. "I was married for many years, but my husband wasn't an accomplished lover. We were high school sweethearts and even though we had three children, we were never what you might call adventurous in our lovemaking. Since his death, I've dated several men, but none of them have had an interest in sex. That was why your ad so intrigued me. I'm not ashamed to admit that I'm a horny old woman. I want the sex that I was denied all my life."

Ian kissed her deeply with such passion that she realized he was right. He didn't need sex toys to show her the love that she so craved.

* * * *

The kiss that Ian initiated was one of the most passionate he had ever given or received. He wanted this woman in every sexual way, but the thought of using the little whip she'd bought or even spanking her was out of the question.

"Are you certain you still want to be my slave, even if I don't beat you?" he asked once they broke their embrace.

"I want you in every way that you can be with me."

"Good, then what I require is that you teach me about this oral sex. It is new to me and I desire to learn all of the tricks of this time and place."

When she took his cock in her mouth, he realized what she was doing. The pleasure she called oral sex was what he had experienced many times in the past, but he called it by a different name. She sucked him as he had suckled many other women. Then he came in her mouth and he enjoyed the look on her face. It was possible that the books she read had told her that women enjoyed swallowing a man's seed, but it was evident this was something she had never done in the past. To her credit, she swallowed down the creamy cum and licked his cock to bring the last drop of him into her mouth.

"Did you enjoy it?" she asked, when he pulled her to her feet and then laid her down on the bed.

"Very much. It is something that I have experienced before, only by a different name. You are very adept at the art. I am surprised that your husband did not enjoy your expertise. Rarely have I seen a woman who is able to swallow the cum that flows from my cock when I ejaculate into her mouth."

She smiled at his compliment.

"Now, my little slave, it is my turn to try this oral sex, as you call it, on you." He parted her legs and again gazed upon Emily's swollen clit. Instead of manipulating it with his fingers, he covered it with his lips and began to suckle as she had suckled him earlier. The screams of pleasure that he had brought to her lips the first night they made love were nothing compared to the ones he heard now. While he sucked her, she came two times without him ever entering her. It pleased him to know that even a travel of over five hundred years through time had not diminished his skills as a lover.

Chapter Ten

Keith settled back in the seat of Julie's car. He enjoyed the restaurant she had chosen for their dinner. The bounty of this time still boggled his mind. Tonight they had feasted on pork ribs basted in a delightful raspberry barbecue sauce and enjoyed what she called micro-brewed beer. It was amazing that the restaurant she had chosen had its own brewery partitioned off from the eating area by a glass. It was interesting to watch as they brewed the beer they enjoyed.

On the way to Madison, she had played a tape of the musical they would be watching. She explained that in order for him to enjoy the performance, he should understand the meaning behind the music.

As he had listened to the story of the woman who had plied her trade as a whore to claw her way to the top of the government of a country he'd never heard of, he thought of Athena. People would have called her a whore, but only because they didn't know her as he did. She had been introduced to the life as a sex slave because her mother couldn't stand the thought of drowning her at birth. Had she been born into a different time, perhaps she would have escaped her life in the harem and become a top government official. She certainly had the intelligence to do such a thing.

Rather than dwell on the woman he had left in the past, Keith turned his attention to Julie. She was the woman of his future. After only one date, as she had called it, he decided she could become very important in his life. He knew that he needed to go slowly, especially when it came to lovemaking. Their conversation of last evening had revealed that her love life had been less than satisfactory, leaving her with doubts about her own sexuality.

As far as Keith was concerned, Julie was a very exciting woman. With the right man, she could be completely satisfied with love in the later years of her life.

"We still have plenty of time before the play starts," Julie announced as they pulled away from the restaurant. "Would you like a tour of the city?"

Keith had wanted to see more of the city Julie referred to as the capital of the state of Wisconsin, but he had hesitated in broaching the subject with Julie. Her suggestion was what he had hoped for.

"I would like that very much. I looked at the map and found this city is built on a chain of lakes. From what I have seen so far, the area is very beautiful."

"I think it's beautiful, but of course I'm prejudiced. I was born in Madison and grew up here. As a child I remember being fascinated not only by the free zoo, but also by the Capitol building and the lakes."

Keith marveled at the beauty of this city. The lakes reminded him of the lakes at home, even though the populated area wasn't much to his liking. Instead of the filth of the cities in his time, he enjoyed the cleanliness of this city. Things had changed in the future and he was pleased that they had. As he recalled, he had always stayed away from the press of humanity that passed as cities in his time.

Unlike him, Ian had thrived in the city, although he couldn't see how anyone could stand such a place, having been raised at a fine manor such as the one the McGowan's kept. He knew that Gwain had spoken highly of his family home when he returned, especially of Angus, the uncle who had sent Gwain to Keith and who had raised Ian after Charles' untimely death.

"I have something to ask you," Julie said. They got out of the car and walked across the well-manicured lawn surrounding the lake that glistened in the late afternoon sunlight.

"If it is in my power, I will give you an honest answer," Keith replied.

For a moment, she chewed at her lip as though trying to decide how to put the words together in the proper order. "Emily and I were talking after we went out last night. We both have some questions about you and Ian."

Keith could feel his stomach churn at the prospect of what she was going to ask him. "What kind of questions?"

"You're going to think I've lost my mind, but are the two of you time travelers? I used to think that such things were only in the books that Emily insists I read. After meeting you, I'm beginning to wonder if they're true."

Keith took Julie's hand in his. "I know it's hard to believe. I have trouble with it myself, but it's true. I gave up wealth, position, and a woman who was one of the best lovers in the world to come to this time and place in search of my nephew. He disappeared without a trace. I missed him terribly and decided that I must find him. When I finally went to the old hag who had sent him here, she told me that if I wanted to follow him, I would never have to worry about finances. She also predicted that another young man would make this journey and that together we would go in search of Gwain. I doubted what she said, but when Ian arrived, I knew she was right."

"You speak of a lover. Are you looking for a lover in this time and place?"

Keith nodded. "I think I have found one in you. It is not often that I can speak of great theatre and literature with a woman. I should know. I had several lovers before I found Athena. I was grieving the loss of my wife, Mary Kate, and soon learned that a woman with beauty was commonplace, but one with a mind that matches mine is rare. Athena, like you, was a rarity. Unfortunately, for all of her intellect, she did not enjoy the literature or art that gave me so much pleasure. I won't push you, but eventually we will become more than friends. We will become lovers, and when that happens I will show you what it's like to be loved by a man of experience." He knew his words had shocked her, but there was no sense in lying.

"What is the year that you came from?" she asked, looking him directly in the eye.

"Gwain returned to me from McGowan Manor in 1471. He stayed only a few days before leaving to search for Tabitha. She is the old hag who sent him into the future in search of a woman by the name of

Denise. I sought Tabitha out in 1474 and spent the better part of a year with her before convincing her that I was serious about wanting to find my nephew. That means it was 1475 when I left Scotland and embarked upon this journey."

She nodded. "What about Ian? When did he join you? From the things you've said, you haven't been here that long."

"I was here about a month when my mentor, one of Tabitha's minions, came to me and told me of Ian's quest. He was but a mere child when I left Scotland, but we were both sent to the same time period. The year that he decided to make the journey was 1503. He, like I, had to spend time with Tabitha, so it was 1504 before he actually made the journey."

"You spoke of lovers, and Emily engaged in sex with Ian last night. Was he also a great lover?"

Keith laughed heartily. "If I can believe the things he has told me about his past, he was one of the best. The story goes that Gwain was brought to McGowan Manor in order to get his brother's wife with child. It seems that Ian has the same occupation. He tells me that he taught the young wives of Inverness the joy of sex as well as giving their aging husbands the sons or daughters to be heirs to their fortunes. Being a much younger man, he does have a great sexual appetite. I am hoping that Emily will be able to keep up with him."

Julie smiled at the visual image of the lusty love that Ian and Emily would be sharing in the weeks to come. "I was thinking the same thing about Ian. Emily enjoys sex. Up until now, I never thought she'd find a partner who was as willing as she to explore new avenues of sex."

Keith put his arm around her shoulders and walked closer to the beach that surrounded the lake. He enjoyed the feel of her body close to his. She wasn't the practiced temptress that Athena had been but she was a woman in dire need of a man, just as he was in dire need for the love of a woman.

* * * *

Julie felt a desire she never experienced before when Keith put his arm around her shoulders. She didn't think it was possible, and at this moment she wished they didn't have theatre tickets. She wanted him in her bed and she wanted him now.

"It will be late when the play ends," she said, turning to face him. "I don't know if I'm up to driving back tonight."

"Is something wrong? Do you feel unwell?"

"I feel better than I have in years. I hope you don't think I'm brazen, but I think we should make reservations at one of the hotels here in town. I certainly wouldn't want to drive back when I'm tired and could possibly cause an accident. The theatre isn't far from the Concourse Hotel. We can stop there and get a room before going to the play. That way we won't have to look for a parking place. We can leave the car in the hotel's lot."

"What are you truly saying? Can it be that you want to become my lover tonight?"

She smiled at his question. "It can. I never thought I wanted a man in my life, but I find that I do. I would like to get to know you better and not just for tonight. This is Friday night and if we can arrange for a package at the hotel, I want to spend the weekend with you. I hope you don't think I sound like a slut, but…"

He put his finger to her lips in an attempt to silence her. "There is no reason for you to think ill of yourself. I, too, want to spend more than a few hours in your company, and I definitely want to become your lover."

Julie could feel a blush creeping into her cheeks. In all the years since her husband left her for another woman, she had never wanted the attentions of a man, but Keith was different. He wanted her in his bed and she wanted to be there.

After parking the car on the street, they went into the front lobby to make reservations.

"May I help you?" the young man at the front desk asked.

"We'd like the best accommodations you have," Keith replied.

"The best? Yes, sir. We do have a Jacuzzi suite available, but nothing else."

"Would you have that available for the next two nights?" Keith inquired.

"Yes, sir, we have a package available. In addition to the complimentary continental breakfast, top-shelf cocktails, hors d'oeuvres, and desserts in the Governor's Club Lounge, the package also includes dinner on Saturday evening, as well as tickets to the theatre of your choice for Saturday evening as well."

Julie felt as though she had died and gone to Heaven. Several years ago she remembered having a friend tell her about spending the weekend in one of the special rooms on the private floor of the Concourse Hotel. The luxury was something she never thought she'd be able to afford or enjoy.

"Are you sure?" she asked. "It sounds terribly expensive."

"I can afford it, and no matter what the cost, it will be worth it to spend the weekend with someone as special as you, my dear."

Keith handed the clerk his credit card and took the key from the young man. "We're parked on the street. Can your valet service park our vehicle in your lot while we go to the theatre?"

"Most certainly, sir. Can we call you a cab to get to the theatre?"

"That won't be necessary," Keith answered. "We're attending the performance of *Evita*. My companion has told me the theatre is within walking distance of this hotel. The night air will do us good."

"It isn't always safe for people to be out walking in the evening," the clerk said. "We have a shuttle that will take you over to the theatre and will be there when the performance ends so that you can get back to the hotel safely."

Keith glanced at Julie, the look in his eye one of bewilderment. "The man is right, Keith. This isn't a small town where you can go out walking without worry of anything terrible happening. I'm afraid that Madison has become a town where one has to be careful. I think it's wonderful that the hotel is willing to supply us with transportation for this evening's performance."

She knew that Keith worried about the thought of violence on the streets of Madison, just as she had when she first heard about such things several years ago. She was too used to small town living to be comfortable with the worries that came from being in downtown Madison after dark.

As they drove toward the theatre, Julie thought about Keith mentioning that Gwain had come to find the love of his life in Denise.

Could it be that the man Denise had married so suddenly, whom she called Mac, was in reality Gwain?

The story Julie heard was that Denise had gone to one of those boring dances at the Senior Citizen Center. There, a handsome stranger had approached her and they had embraced as though they were long-lost lovers.

Was it possible that Denise had traveled back to 1470 in order to become Mac's lover? If so, she had been cruelly taken from the man she had loved. It was only a miracle that they had been reunited over five hundred years in the future.

If Mac and Gwain were one and the same, then Keith's reason for coming to the future was within his reach. Would he dump her as soon as she helped him achieve his goal? If so, she refused to tell him what she knew until this weekend was ended.

For the first time in her life, she desired the company of a man who could show her the love she had been denied in the marriage bed she'd shared with her husband. She knew it was selfish, but she didn't care.

This weekend, she planned to find out what it was like to have the sexual experience that Emily lusted after and seemed to have found in Ian's arms.

Chapter Eleven

The music of *Evita* echoed in Keith's head as they left the theatre. It was one thing to hear it from the DVD player in Julie's car and another to experience it in the theatre. The story had been as fresh as everything else he had enjoyed in this new time and place and as old as the profession of prostitution itself.

The main character, Evita, was based on a real person and she had done what it took to not only survive but to also claw her way to one of the top positions in the government of her country. Even though most people would have been appalled at the thought of anyone doing such things, he stood in awe of a woman who was able to gain such power from what she did in the bedroom.

Outside, there were numerous taxis and limos waiting for people to pay the fare they demanded to take them to their homes or hotels. Among those waiting was a van with the name of the Concourse Hotel printed on the door.

"Mr. Fletcher?" the driver inquired.

Keith nodded and allowed Julie to enter the open door of the van ahead of him. As he did, he remembered when he had visited the city and stayed with wealthy friends. They had a driver for their coach who was as courteous as this man when he picked them up from whatever party they had attended.

"The play was fantastic," Julie purred as she snuggled close to him. "I'd heard how wonderful it was and I've seen the movie, but nothing could compare to what we saw tonight."

"I hope what I have planned for the rest of the weekend will be equally enjoyable for you."

She clasped his arm tighter. He couldn't help but wonder if she was looking forward to the lovemaking they would enjoy, or if she was scared to death. She'd told him that she wasn't interested in sex but was that the truth? At the time he decided it was, but somewhere along the line she had changed her mind. It was possible that the attraction was that he came from another time and place. He hoped it was more than that, for she reminded him so much of Mary Kate that he was certain she was the reincarnation of his beloved wife.

The complimentary shuttle left them off at the front door of the hotel. Once in the lobby, Keith followed Julie to the bank of elevators. This was one thing he enjoyed about this time. He didn't relish climbing several flights of stairs to get to the suite they had reserved for the weekend. The elevator was one of the best things that had been invented since his time period.

"To get to our floor, you have to put your key into this slot," Julie instructed.

Keith watched as Julie slid the plastic key that reminded him of a credit card into the slot next to the buttons that had the various floors printed on them. After the card was accepted, she pushed the button for one of the top floors that were marked Governor's Club Executive Level.

As usual, when the elevator began its assent to the upper floors, Keith felt his stomach drop. The first time he had experienced it, he had thought it a strange sensation. Now that he was used to it, he anticipated the rush of excitement it brought on.

Once the elevator stopped at their floor, they started down the hall toward the corner room with the number that matched the key they'd been given at the desk.

The sitting room of the suite was as grand as any of the houses of his elite friends in the city. Plush carpeting covered the floor and the furnishings were considerably more expensive than the ones in his condo. Off to one side was a small kitchenette and across the room a doorway led to the bedroom.

"This is so much better than any hotel I've ever stayed in," Julie said, her voice hardly louder than a soft whisper. "I can't believe that we're here for the entire weekend."

He pulled her into his embrace. "It's nothing more than you deserve."

She softened for a moment, and then pulled away. "I just thought of something. We have nothing to wear tomorrow and no toiletries. I don't even have a nightgown."

Keith chuckled. "You don't need a nightgown, for I would just have to remove it. As for the rest, there is nothing saying that we can't go shopping for anything we need in the morning. For tonight, I only plan to enjoy this beautiful woman who has agreed to spend the weekend with me."

"I–I know I agreed to come but..."

"But what, Julie?"

She shook her head and turned away from him. "I never enjoyed sex with my husband. I know that Emily tells me I don't know what I'm missing, but I know what I had with my husband and I'm afraid I won't know what to do."

With her back to him he could see her shake as silent sobs wracked her body. In the hope of consoling her, he put his hands on her shoulders. "Sex, my dear Julie, is as natural as breathing. I have been blessed that my partners have been receptive, but I have heard of others who are not so lucky. In my time I heard many stories about how the wives of the crofters who lived upon my land were disappointed in their marriage beds. They would tell my wife things that were never meant for my ears. The biggest complaints that I heard were that the men rushed their lovemaking and were rough in bed. They forgot that they were with women and not the men who enjoyed rough play. My wife often suggested that I talk to them, but it was not something that men discussed."

Slowly, Julie again turned back to him. "I can understand that. I could never talk to my husband about what I wanted or how I thought I should be treated. It seemed if things weren't done his way, they weren't done correctly. When things got so bad I couldn't stand it any longer, I asked him for a divorce. He certainly didn't argue with me and gave me everything I wanted. I think he was anxious to be rid of me and my complaints."

It seemed entirely natural for him to slip his arms around her waist and pull her close to him. "Well, my sweet, tonight you are in for a lesson in loving the way it was meant to be. We have the entire weekend to get to know each other in the way a man knows a woman, and I plan to take advantage of all my expertise to make you feel comfortable until you are ready to complete the ultimate act of love."

He could feel her relax in his arms. If he went slowly and maintained his patience, he was certain they would be making love until the sun crested the Eastern horizon.

* * * *

Julie allowed Keith to follow her into the ornate bathroom. Once in there, she flipped the switch on the wall that ran the whirlpool. She knew it would take a few minutes for the water to heat. While it did, her stomach began to churn. *We'll be using the whirlpool in the nude. Am I ready for this man to see my body?*

As though it were the most natural thing in the world, Keith took off his shirt, displaying a chest of red hair that was peppered with golden highlights. Intermingled with the gold were several strands of silver that denoted he wasn't a young man any longer. Instead of turning her off, she reached out to entangle her fingers in the thick mat of hair that surrounded his male nipples.

She remembered her husband taking off his shirt in front of her. He never had much chest hair and when she wanted to touch his nipples, he always stopped her. He said it wasn't natural for a woman to play with a man's tits. Those pleasures were for men only. After that, he would manipulate her breasts until they ached from the pain of his rough treatment. The memory caused her to quickly take her hands from his chest.

"Is something wrong?" he asked as he caught her wrists in his hands and held them loosely.

"Men don't like to have women touch them there," she replied.

"Whatever gave you such an idea? My nipples are as sensitive as yours and when you pay attention to them, it arouses me."

"My husband…"

"Now listen to me," he said softly. "I'm not your husband and I hope I never meet him. I cannot believe that he has wronged you so badly. What he told you was his personal opinion. Not all men are like him, and I am certainly one that is different. I have a feeling no man has ever made love to you. Instead, they have fucked you."

She swallowed hard. How often has she thought the same thing herself? The lovemaking that Emily described so often was nothing like what she had experienced in her life. She couldn't remember ever having an orgasm. In reality, when it came to lovemaking, she was a virtual virgin.

He loosened his grip on her wrists and guided her hands back to his chest. Tentatively, she ran her fingers through the soft hairs until she rested them on his nipples. They immediately pebbled beneath her touch. As they did, she wondered what it would be like if a man did the same for her, rather than roughly grope and squeeze her breasts before biting her nipples until she cried with pain.

His response to her manipulations of his nipples was to pull her into his tight embrace and kiss her with an urgency she'd never experienced before. Rather than puckering his lips as though he was blowing up a balloon, he kissed her with an open mouth and sucked at her bottom lip before slipping his tongue into her waiting mouth.

This was the kind of kiss she saw in the movies and on television and the reaction it produced was surprising. Rather than just a kiss, it was one that made her insides quiver and wetness pool in her panties. Never in her life had a kiss done that to her. She was glad she had decided to spend the night and give herself completely to this man who so easily had aroused something that she thought never existed.

* * * *

Keith enjoyed being the man to awaken Julie's sexuality. As for her husband, he prayed he never crossed paths with the man because if he did, he would either have to kill or castrate him.

Her fingers on his chest had brought erotic ideas to his mind that were downright sinful. Carefully, he unbuttoned her blouse in order to gaze upon her soft white mounds. Once he did, he smiled at the beautiful lace bra she wore. After watching numerous movies on the television, he knew all about women's undergarments in this time and place.

Her breasts were not the small ones of the actresses in the movies, they were full and heavy with the maturity her age denoted. She was a woman he could come to love and love with all the gentleness Athena had taught him and Mary Kate had desired.

He slipped his hands behind her and unhooked the bra. As he did, he gazed over her shoulder and was surprised to see an artistic little butterfly drawn on the back of her left shoulder. Having never seen anything like this, he turned her around in order to examine it more closely.

"This butterfly is beautiful, but why would you draw it upon your skin?"

"It's a tattoo," she replied. "It was something I never wanted, but my husband told me it would make me sexier to him. I was foolish enough to believe him. The pain of it was overpowering, but at the time I was more interested in saving a marriage that had died a less-than-honorable death than in my own wishes."

"Then for that one thing, I am eternally grateful to this man who has caused you so much pain and taken away your desire for sex. I think it is beautiful and enhances your beauty. My only regret is the pain it caused you when it was placed upon your body."

He carefully traced the butterfly and was surprised that it felt no different than the rest of her skin. Once he satisfied his curiosity, he kissed the delicate piece of art in adoration of its beauty. As he did, he felt her shiver. He knew it wasn't because she was cold, but because the feel of his lips on her shoulder excited her until she was almost ready to lose control.

Before turning her back to face him, he unbuttoned her skirt and slid down the zipper so that it could pool around her ankles. As he did, he was surprised to see that she wore panties, but the hose that encased her legs was not the kind that came with panties. Since her skirt came to her mid-calf, she wore ones that reminded him of the socks worn by the men of this time. The difference was that they were sheer and came all the way to her knees held in place with a wide elastic band.

Without making comment, he slipped her panties from her body, marveling at the swell of her ass. Her bottom was well rounded and fit in his hands perfectly, but there would be time enough for him to enjoy that pleasure once they were in bed together. For now, there was more of her he wanted to explore.

Moving around in front of her, he gazed upon her naked breasts, and his arousal became almost painful at the sight of them. Below that was not the flat stomach of the women on the television, but that of a woman who was mature and had enjoyed her life.

He shifted his gaze to the soft hair that hid her womanly pleasures. He longed to plunge his cock deep within her folds, but he knew there would be time for that later. Tonight was the time for her to experience the joy rather than the pain of their lovemaking.

"You are so beautiful; I don't know how I got so lucky. In my life, there have been only three women who were special to me. The first was my wife, Mary Kate—she was beautiful and fiercely independent. She gave me beautiful children and died far too young. The next was my lover, Athena. She was a well-trained courtesan and taught me the beauty of lovemaking. Now there is you. Tonight, I will be the teacher and you the recipient of the love I want to show you."

Without waiting for her reply, Keith wrapped Julie in his arms and again kissed her with the urgency he had felt as a youth. Her response was to kiss him back and slip her tongue within the cavern of his mouth to do battle with his. The taste of her was sweet and inviting.

He didn't hesitate, but merely picked her up and carried her into the bathroom where the whirlpool bubbled with steam rising from it. He set her on her feet and invited her to step into the tub of water.

"What about you?" she asked.

"I will join you as soon as I finish undressing. This is one pleasure I have heard about and want to try."

After she stepped into the water, he took off his pants. Freed from the restrictions of his underwear, his cock sprang to life. From the expression on her face, she was pleased with the sight of his rock hardness.

Holding out her hand to him, he too stepped into the water and enjoyed the warmth that spread throughout his body. The only thing that he could equate it to was the hot baths that Athena prepared for him. The problem was that the water cooled too quickly. From what he had seen on television, these hot tubs did not cool, but continued to be hot for the entire time the bathers were immersed in its bubbling waters.

Once he seated himself on the built-in seats around the edge of the tub, he glanced over at Julie. Her eyes were closed and there was a delightful smile on her lips. "This is heavenly," she murmured.

Before he could reply, she reached out and took his cock in her hands. "I've only ever been with one man, and from what I saw when you took off your pants, he was nothing more than a little boy. I've seen pictures in magazines, but no one I've ever seen could begin to compare to you."

He smiled as she wrapped her fingers around him. As though it had a mind of its own, his cock began to pulse and grow even bigger than it had been only moments earlier. It groaned for him to give it the relief it craved, but he knew he had to go slowly with Julie. There was no need to frighten her before he gave her all the pleasure she deserved.

Trying to ignore his own needs, he ran his fingers through her woman's hair and then into the moist valley of her pussy. He immediately found the nub of her clit and massaged it until she cried out in pleasure. Like his cock responded to Julie's touch, her clit grew under his fingers.

"What are you doing to me?" she questioned, the word coming out as a moan of pleasure.

"This is called foreplay. I don't have to ask if your husband ever did such things to you, because he undoubtedly thought only of his own pleasure and not of yours. Just relax, for there is more to come before this night is over."

He felt her relax under his fingers and once she did, he slid them into her cunt. The walls surrounding them were tight and as soon as he had three fingers inside her, she began to pulse in the same manner as his cock had done earlier.

It took her only a moment to come to climax. With her warm juices running over his fingers, he knew he needed to be inside her to more fully enjoy the beauty of this moment.

She moved, giving him complete access to her. She opened her legs and within the warm water, he slowly inserted his cock into her welcoming shaft. The surprise in her eyes as she adjusted to him being inside her brought a smile to his lips. That, combined with the feeling against his cock, brought him to full arousal.

At first he pumped against her slowly, but once she adjusted to his size and he became more aroused, he pumped faster. When he could no longer restrain himself, he came with a might he had never before experienced. Perhaps it was because with his travels through time, he hadn't had sex in over five hundred years.

* * * *

Julie couldn't believe her reaction to the remarkable sex she had just enjoyed with Keith. His gentle foreplay had led up to the most beautiful experience in her life. After what she just experienced, she knew she had never really made love to a man in her life. Instead, her husband's attempts were for his own enjoyment and gratification. In doing so, he had only fucked her.

What surprised her even more was her reaction to what they just did. For the first time in her life, she experienced an orgasm. She couldn't help but wonder that if she told Keith about Denise's new husband, Mac, would Keith no longer need her, no longer make her feel like a real woman.

She put all thoughts of the future behind her as she allowed Keith to help her out of the miniature hot tub and wrap her in the complimentary robe that came with the room. The terry cloth of the robe surrounded her in warmth and absorbed the droplets of water that clung to her skin. The comfort of this luxury was multiplied when Keith wrapped her in the additional warmth of his embrace.

"Being with you was one of the most exhilarating experiences of my life," Keith whispered in her ear. "I hope it was as good for you."

Julie clung to him tightly. "It was—it was the most wonderful thing I've ever experienced in my life," she managed to say before bursting into tears.

To her dismay, Keith pulled away from their embrace and held her at arm's length. "Julie, what is it about our lovemaking that brings tears to your eyes? Did I hurt you?"

She shook her head no. "It's not that. I never thought that I would be able to experience what my friends have talked about for years. You've made that all possible, but there is something I have to tell you and when I do, I'm afraid this will be the last time we'll be together like this."

"There is nothing you could possibly tell me that would drive me from your arms."

"The man you're looking for lives very close to the house I share with Emily."

"Gwain? Do you mean that Gwain is someone you know? I don't understand, you said you didn't know him. How could you lie about something that is so important to me?"

Julie stepped further away from Keith before turning away from him completely. She couldn't stand the look of condemnation in his eyes. She hadn't lied to him, not really. The name Gwain had meant nothing to her. It wasn't until Keith had mentioned Denise that the bells had gone off in her head.

She knew she should have told him as soon as she realized who he was looking for, but if she had, she would have never experienced the beauty of the lovemaking they had just shared.

"I–I didn't lie to you," she began, still unable to acknowledge the look of betrayal in his eyes. "I didn't know who you were looking for until you mentioned Denise earlier this evening. I was selfish enough to have wanted to enjoy the remainder of our evening before I told you."

"Why would you not know about him?"

"He doesn't go by the name of Gwain. The only name I've ever heard him called was Mac. I suppose when they were married, he used his given name, but they eloped and were married in Las Vegas. None of Denise's friends attended the wedding, although we all went to the reception that was held at the Senior Citizen Center. That was where they met."

"I don't understand. What is this Senior Citizen Center that you speak of?"

Still unable to meet his gaze, Julie refused to turn back to face him. "It used to be the library in town, but when the new one was built it was given to the older citizens of the city as a place to gather and socialize. I had heard there was a new man in town, but the first time he came to the weekly dance, I had other plans. The story goes that he approached Denise and the rest, as they say, is history. Within weeks they were married, and they were the talk of the town for months after that. They've been married for about a year now and the way they carry on you'd think they were just a couple of kids rather than sexy senior citizens."

"In comparison to me, he is but a young man," Keith said, putting his hands on her upper arms.

She shuddered, waiting for him to say it was time for them to get dressed and return home, so that he could find the nephew he had traveled through time to locate. "What do you mean?"

"When Gwain left Scotland he wasn't much older than Ian. He was the man I had planned to leave my lands to, as well as my wealth. It was his choice to come to this time and place as a man the same age as Denise. I found that hard to believe, but I am certain he wanted to love her as her equal in age. I was given no such choice and for that I am pleased. I doubt you would have agreed to be with me if I were as young as Ian."

"Do–do you still want to be with me?"

"Why wouldn't I want to be with a woman who has given me as much satisfaction as both Athena and Mary Kate put together?"

"I–I thought…"

He turned her to face him. "Did you think that once I found the man I came in search of that I would give up the pleasures of the woman I have only just met? Nothing could be further from the truth. The loving I have planned for you has only begun. We are here for the entire weekend and I don't plan to waste a moment of that time. If I continue to be lucky, you will agree to be not only my lover, but also my wife. You are not the kind of woman who would be with a man without the benefit of marriage. I have had sex in both ways, and I know that I enjoy the permanent relationship of marriage to that of being with a lover. Athena did not think the same way. I asked her to be my wife on more than one occasion, but she always turned me down."

Julie blinked several times, trying to comprehend exactly what Keith had just said. "Did you just ask me to marry you?"

Keith nodded. "I see in you the woman who once held my heart in her hands. If I am not mistaken, you are the reincarnation of my beloved Mary Kate and as such, you are the woman I was destined to fall in love with over and over again throughout all eternity."

Julie felt weak in the knees. She had only known Keith for a few days and yet she could easily imagine spending the remainder of her life with him. It wasn't just the sex. She had been immediately attracted to him and now she was beginning to understand. It was entirely possible that she was the reincarnation of Keith's dead wife. If so, maybe there was some truth to being connected to the same people throughout eternity. In the past she had heard psychics saying that people married the reincarnations of their true loves over and over again.

"I couldn't find another man who would be a better partner for life. I feel like I've known you forever and if you want me, I would be thrilled to be your wife."

Keith's smile spoke volumes. "As soon as I find Gwain, we will make plans to be married. I want him by my side when I take you as my wife. For now, there is a bed waiting for us to begin practicing for the wedding night."

Julie felt as though the years of her life had fallen away and she was again a young woman in love with the idea of being in love. The only difference was this time she was with a man who enjoyed giving her the pleasure she deserved.

* * * *

Keith could hardly believe that he had voiced his desire to make Julie his wife in such a way. He knew the first night he met her that she was the reincarnation of his first wife. Reincarnation was the only explanation for the uncanny resemblance between Mary Kate and Julie.

His suspicions were confirmed when he made love to her. As soon as he entered her body, he knew she had been Mary Kate in another lifetime. Making love to her the first time had been like taking Mary

Kate's virginity many lifetimes ago. The fact they had found each other again was almost unbelievable. A love like this did not happen for a man more than once in his lifetime. The very thought that he had traversed time and space in order to find it brought a smile to his lips. Without Gwain's travels, in order to find the woman who controlled his heart, he would have missed out on this experience entirely.

Following his suggestion, Julie made her way to the bed and he followed. He needed to show her how much he loved and needed her. He hoped that the travel through time had not diminished his stamina where lovemaking was concerned.

In the bedroom, he helped her take off the robe and expose her body to him again. Even though he had enjoyed her delights and seen her body previously, the effect on him was overpowering. He longed to gaze on her cunt and view what he had only felt while they were in the whirlpool.

To his surprise, he saw Julie stifle a yawn. The action, no matter how small, reminded him that he was no longer the young man who had loved Mary Kate with abandon. He wasn't even the middle-aged man who had fallen for the sexual charms of Athena. As a man with grown children and grandchildren, he realized that he needed his rest. They had an entire weekend for the pleasures he had in mind for Julie. For now they both needed to sleep, content in each other's arms.

"I have enjoyed your delights to the fullest extent," he said as he pulled her into his arms and held her close. "The problem is that I am no longer a young man with unlimited stamina."

Julie smiled. "I was hoping you would come to that conclusion. I need my rest and I think you do as well. We have the entire weekend to continue these explorations. I'm certain our sweet dreams will lead to even sweeter lovemaking when we are more rested."

Chapter Twelve

Emily awoke in Ian's embrace. Their night of lovemaking had left her drained and she'd slept better than she had in months.

"Good morning, beautiful." Ian said, as he pulled her closer for their first kiss of the morning.

"It is a good morning. As much as I want to make love to you again, I need a shower."

"I was going to suggest the same thing, followed by breakfast. I'm starving. Are you up to going out to the restaurant for something to eat?"

Emily thought for a moment before answering Ian's question. It would be tempting to spend the entire day in bed, but hunger clawed at her stomach. "I think that's a wonderful idea. Let's start with the shower and then go out."

Before she could step into the shower, her cell phone began to ring. "You go ahead and get the water the right temperature and I'll join you as soon as I take this call. It could be from Julie. I'm dying to know how her evening with Keith ended."

Ian laughed at her. "Women do not change no matter what the century. There is not one that I have ever met who couldn't resist hearing gossip about their friends. I will be lonely in the shower, but you do need to answer the phone."

Emily nodded and retrieved the phone from her purse. To her surprise, when she checked the caller ID she saw that it was Denise McGowan on the other end of the line.

"Good Morning," Emily said in greeting.

"Hi, Emily. I'm sure your caller ID told you who's calling. I've been trying to reach Julie, but I'm not getting an answer at the house and I didn't want to leave a message on her cell."

"Oh, she went on a date last night. She told me they were going to Madison to see *Evita*. It's possible that she got home late enough that she turned off the ringer so that she could sleep in. Is there something I can help you with?"

"To be truthful, yes, there is. We've heard that Julie is seeing a man by the name of Keith Fletcher. Mac is certain this man is his uncle."

Emily's mind raced. Ian and Keith had told them that they were looking for the same man, Gwain McGowan. At the time, the name hadn't meant anything. There were a lot of people of Scottish decent in the area and McGowan was a common name. She realized that Mac and Gwain could be one in the same.

"What's Mac's first name?" she finally asked. "I don't think I've ever heard you call him anything but Mac."

Denise hesitated for a moment. "It's Gwain. He doesn't go by it because of all the teasing he gets about the Gwain from *King Arthur and the Knights of the Round Table*. Why do you ask?"

"I was just wondering. Julie isn't the only one who has a new man in her life. I've met a wonderful man by the name of Ian Brice. He and Keith are good friends. I'll see if he knows anything about Mac."

"I'd appreciate that. Mac is anxious to learn if Keith is indeed his uncle. It's been a long time since he's seen his family."

Emily closed the phone. Could Denise's new husband be a time traveler like Ian and Keith? Gwain McGowan was the man they were seeking, but could she bring herself to tell Ian where to find him? If they were to meet, would it be the end of the relationship that had brought her some of the most wonderful sex she'd enjoyed in years?

Absently, she started slipping the phone into her purse when she noticed that she had a message. Her curiosity made her open the phone again and check the message. At least it would take her mind off the call from Denise and the realization that sooner or later she was going to have to tell Ian about Gwain McGowan.

"Hi Em," Julie's voice greeted her. *"I didn't want you to worry. I'm spending the weekend in Madison with Keith. This may be my last*

chance, because I figured out who Keith and Ian are looking for. Keith said that Gwain came in search of Denise. It has to be Denise McGowan's husband, Mac. I'm afraid that when I tell him, he'll leave me, so I intend to enjoy this weekend to the fullest. I'll see you Sunday night."

Emily closed the phone. It was Saturday morning and she had less than thirty-six hours to enjoy Ian. Once Julie and Keith returned home, the truth would be out. Once they told Keith and Ian they knew where to find Gwain, the relationships they were enjoying could easily fall apart before their eyes.

I don't want that to happen. I wonder if there's a way I can keep Ian in my life once I tell him the truth.

She shook her head to rid herself of the distressing thoughts. More than anything else, she wanted to prolong the pleasure she had found with Ian. She hurried to the bathroom, and after hearing the water running, she opened the door to the shower and stepped inside the enclosure to join Ian under the spray of hot water.

"I didn't think you'd ever get here," Ian greeted her. "Of course, I understand how women are when they talk with their friends."

"The call from my friend didn't last all that long, but there was a message from Julie. It seems that Keith has agreed to spend the weekend in Madison with her. I may have misjudged my friend. Maybe she is more interested in sex than I thought. She sounded happier than she has in months."

"From what I hear, Keith can make her happy. I knew of his lover, Athena. She was one of the best madams in Scotland with more than one suitor who swore by the way she made love. It was because of Keith's generosity that she was able to open her house and give pleasure to many men."

Emily could feel tears prickling at the back of her eyes. Keith could easily teach Julie to be a woman again, but would he leave her and in the process destroy the fragile sexual awakening within her friend?

Ian ran his soapy hands over Emily's body, but instead of the pleasure she had enjoyed earlier, now they brought tears.

"You're crying," Ian observed. "Have I hurt you?"

She shook her head. "No, but I'm afraid that if I tell you about the two phone calls I had, you will put me aside."

* * * *

Emily's words cut Ian like a knife. How could what she learned on the phone affect him enough to not want her in his bed or in his life? He allowed the water to wash the soapy residue from their bodies. Once they were clean, he wrapped her in one of the fluffy bath sheets that were stocked in the linen closet of his bathroom.

As much as he wanted to pay homage to her tits as well as her cunt, he refrained. His touch had brought tears to her eyes and he couldn't take the chance of that happening again.

"Now, what's this all about?" he asked once they were dressed and ready to leave for the restaurant.

"I know you came to this time to find a man named Gwain. I also know that you advertised for an older woman because that was the age of the woman Gwain sought when he came to this time. I honestly didn't have any idea who he was until I heard from my friend, Denise McGowan."

The name McGowan echoed in Ian's mind. The story he heard from both William and Tabitha had included the name of Denise as the woman who had changed places with William's mother in order to make love to Gwain and give birth to the son her husband, Charles, desired.

If Denise McGowan was the one Gwain had sought, it was entirely possible that he had found the love of his life and was living close enough for Ian to find him for William. Since Tabitha had told him there was no way he could return to his own time, just telling Gwain about his son was his mission.

In the process of coming to this time, he had met a woman who was an exciting lover. It was true that she was older than him and he'd never had an older lover, but if the truth were known, he was centuries older than she.

"Are you telling me you have found Gwain?" he asked.

Emily's tears flowed faster. "I didn't realize he was who you were looking for because he goes by the name of Mac."

"Help me to understand why you are crying."

"Once you find Gwain..." She stopped, sniffing loudly. "You'll have no use for me. I don't want to lose you."

Ian smiled and then laughed out loud. "Do you think the only reason I've made love to you is to find Gwain?"

She nodded her answer to his question.

"I am hardly that shallow. I have had sex with many women in my life, but I have made love to only a select few. You are one of those women, and the thought of losing you just because I have found Gwain is one that never crossed my mind. I think your hunger has clouded your mind. Once we have eaten our fill, I will show you that finding Gwain does not dampen my desire for you."

* * * *

Relief flooded Emily's mind. This was supposed to be a romp but it had turned into so much more. The last thing she ever expected was to fall in love with this man. After their two nights of lovemaking, she realized he was someone she wanted in her life. To have him tell her the same thing was one of the best things she could have hoped to hear.

After breakfast they took a leisurely walk, looking in many of the shop windows before returning to his condo to enjoy each other further. They no more than entered the living room when he took her in his arms and kissed her with an urgency that hadn't been there before.

"Does this tell you how much you mean to me, Emily?" he asked.

"I want it to. Just in case you change your mind, make love to me, Ian."

It surprised her when he picked her up and carried her into his bedroom. Once he laid her on the bed, he slipped off her shoes and socks. She thought he was going to take off her jeans and underwear, but instead he started massaging her right foot. She shivered with excitement as he found erotic zones she never knew existed. When she didn't think things could get any better, he began sucking on her toes.

The orgasms she had experienced so many times in the past two days were nothing in comparison to the one that came over her as she gave into the pleasure of his attentions.

Chapter Thirteen

On Sunday, Ian insisted they go to church and then over to Emily's house to search for information on the Internet about William McGowan. "Here it is," Emily exclaimed. "There's even a picture of him."

> *William Wallace McGowan was born in 1471, the son of Charles McGowan. When William was five years of age, his father Charles was killed by his friend, Brian Graham. In retaliation, Angus McGowan, Charles' uncle, killed Brian and took on the task of raising William.*
>
> *At the age of twenty-six, William entered politics and along with running McGowan Manor, was a well-known man in parliament. His fame spread as far as London and Paris and he served for a while as a diplomat to France.*
>
> *Having fathered six children, it is rumored that he was an exceptional lover who outlived two wives. He also cared for his mother Davida, until her death in 1506.*

"The picture is a good drawing of him," Ian commented. "Angus always said that he resembled his father closely. I could never see the resemblance myself. Of course, at the time I didn't realize that Charles wasn't his true father. Does he favor Gwain?"

Emily stared at the picture for several moments before answering. "It's remarkable; they could be brothers rather than father and son. Was he really a politician?"

"He was only starting his political career when I left Inverness, but I am certain he was good at whatever he did. The article says he was a great lover, and that is no exaggeration. He did outlive two wives, but that didn't count the number of lovers who graced his bed. I was older than William and became sexually active with the crofter's daughters when I was but thirteen. It didn't take long for William to join me when I went into the village to see my young lovers. I doubt there is a woman in the village that didn't enjoy his cock when she was younger."

"You were only thirteen? In this time, most boys aren't mature enough for sex that early. I, on the other hand, lost my virginity at the age of fourteen. It was a wonderful experience, but I have to admit everyone thought I was a bit of a slut."

Ian laughed heartily. "You, a slut? Never. You are a very sexual person. It is a shame I did not meet you before you lost your virginity. It would have been my pleasure to take that from you."

He returned his attention to the computer screen. "Do you think we might be able to find something about Keith in this machine?"

Emily nodded. "You said he was a wealthy landowner. It's entirely possible that there are things about him. Let's see."

Ian watched as she typed in Keith's name. To his surprise, a portrait of the man he had come to call a friend appeared on the screen. He read with interest the story that had been written about him.

Keith Fletcher was born in 1415 on the family manor in the Scottish Highlands. A wealthy man, he disappeared in 1475, leaving his manor to his grandson, Jamie McDonald. The manor, now a historical village, is still owned by the McDonald family and has always been referred to as Fletcher Manor.

His long time mistress, Athena, went on to become a famous madam in Inverness, pleasuring many men with her exotic talents. She died in 1510 after having only one child, a son by the name of Keith, who it is rumored belonged to Keith Fletcher. He became a wealthy man after taking over the business of well-known wool merchant, Ian Brice, who also disappeared under suspicious circumstances.

After reading the words about him, Ian wondered if he would find more about himself on the Internet. "Could we type in my name and see what comes up?" he asked Emily.

Before he finished the question, she had already typed his name into the inquiry box. It took only a moment for several sites to come up. The first one proved to be the most interesting.

It was rumored that Ian Brice of Inverness met with foul play when he disappeared in 1508. According to his cousin, well-known politician, William McGowan, the last he heard of Ian was when he left on a personal quest. William said he was certain there had been no foul play.

In contrast was the declaration that Ian had fathered several children for wealthy men in the city of Inverness. The most well-know of these children was named for him. Ian Brice Galbraith became famous for his connection with William McGowan. Working as a clerk in McGowan's office, he took over his office when McGowan passed away suddenly in 1530 of a heart attack.

Tears sprung to Ian's eyes. He knew that everyone he knew and loved in the past was long dead, but reading it made the pain of loss real. In his mind William was a vibrant man, not a dead one.

"It's hard to read about the loss of a friend, isn't it?" Emily asked as she closed the window with the information about William's death.

Ian nodded and then took her hand in his. "I can think of more pleasurable things for us to be doing,"

She got to her feet and allowed him to pull her into a tight embrace. She was right, it had been hard to read about the loss of William, but the actual event had happened almost four hundred and seventy-five years in the past. This was his present and he couldn't change anything that had happened in another lifetime. Had he stayed in Inverness rather than going on the quest for William, he too would be long dead and would never have had the pleasure he found within the confines of Emily's arms. In leaving when he did, he had been blessed with the miracles of the twenty-first century.

"Is anyone home?" they heard Julie call, breaking them apart.

"We're in the office," Emily replied. "We'll be right out."

Ian hesitated for a moment. He knew that Keith was anxious to find Gwain, but had Julie found the words to tell him? Also, how would he feel about knowing that there was still a manor that carried his name and it had become a tourist attraction? Ian knew that the realization that one of his offspring carried his name had been strangely rewarding. He decided that he would go back to the computer and see if he could find any descendents of Ian Brice Galbraith. Even if they wouldn't believe that he had traveled through time and was their ancestor, it would be good to meet them.

* * * *

Julie knew that Emily would be apprehensive about telling Ian that she knew where to find Gwain McGowan. She prayed that Ian's reaction would be as responsive as Keith's had been.

With Keith by her side, she glanced again at the diamond ring that graced the third finger of her left hand. Never in her wildest dreams had she thought she would ever remarry, but in one weekend Keith had changed her mind completely. As soon as he was reunited with Gwain, they would begin planning their wedding, including a trip back to Scotland so that he could see all the things that had changed in his homeland since he left.

When Emily entered the room, it was evident that she had been well loved this weekend.

"Did you have a good time?" Emily asked, coming to Julie's side.

"It was wonderful. I have something to tell you." Rather than saying anything more, she held up her hand to show off the engagement ring.

"You're getting married?" Emily inquired before taking Julie in her arms and giving her a hug. "Have you told him about Mac?" she whispered.

"Yes. Have you told Ian?"

Emily nodded. Julie let out a sigh of relief. Everything would be easier from here on out with the truth about Gwain McGowan out in the open.

"Can you believe it?" Keith asked. "Not only have I found the man I loved as a son, I have found the reincarnation of my first wife, Mary Kate."

"Have you met Gwain?" Ian questioned.

"Not yet. Since we have come on the same quest, I thought it only fitting that we should both meet him at the same time."

Emily was thrilled to know that the cat was out of the bag. Now was the time for them to make plans for the reunion that had brought Keith and Ian on their journey across the centuries to enjoy.

* * * *

Keith held his breath and he knew Ian was doing the same. Emily had put the phone on 'speaker' so they could all hear what was being said on the other end. The problem was that it had now rung three times and no one had answered.

"Hello," a man answered, his voice laced with a thick Scottish brogue.

Even though it had been several years since he had heard Gwain's voice, Keith knew he would have recognized it anywhere.

"Gwain," Keith said, his own voice hardly more than a hoarse whisper. "Is it possible that I'm really talking to you?"

"Uncle Keith? I heard you were here, but I didn't know if I should believe it. How did you..."

"I found the old hag who sent you here and bribed her to do the same for me. My friend Ian did the same as a favor for your son, William. We've been here for several weeks, but didn't know how to find you. If it weren't for Emily and Julie, we'd still be looking for you."

He looked up to see both women with tears in their eyes. It had amazed him to learn that Julie was worried that he would leave her once he found Gwain. Nothing could be further from the truth. In fact, he had found so much more on this adventure that he thanked God every day for his good fortune. When Mary Kate died, he knew a bit of his heart had been scarred beyond repair. Now that he had once again found her, he had no intentions of ever letting go of the woman who made him complete.

With the ice broken, Ian took over the conversation. It didn't take long for the three couples to plan a meeting. Even though Emily fussed that the house wasn't clean enough for company, Gwain—or Mac as everyone here called him—and Denise, promised they would arrive in less than fifteen minutes.

Keith was so overjoyed at the prospect that he wanted to take Julie in his arms and make delightful love to her, but instead she bustled around picking things up and helping Emily to prepare snacks.

"Can you believe it?" Ian asked. "In a few minutes, we will see Gwain. I don't know if I'll even know him."

"Of course you will. You showed me that portrait of William on the computer and he looks exactly like Gwain when he was that age. I doubt either of us will have a problem knowing the man who is coming here."

"You love him like a son, don't you?"

Keith nodded. "When Gwain was fostered to me, he was the son Mary Kate and I couldn't produce. We both loved him fiercely. By the time Charles called him back to McGowan Manor to give him a son, we had shared more than most fathers and sons share. It was my idea for Athena to teach him how to love a woman with his whole heart."

"It must have been a blow when he went in search of Denise."

"It was, but like any good father, I knew he had to learn about life on his own. I made arrangements to leave my holdings to my grandson, and within three years I was ready to follow him. Now I will get to see Gwain again and my excitement is growing with each passing minute."

"What about Julie? Do you really intend to marry her?"

"What you don't understand is that I've found more than Gwain. I'm positive that Julie is the reincarnation of my late wife, Mary Kate.

She's been waiting here for me and I for her. We will have a wonderful life together."

Before Ian could answer, the doorbell rang. Both men turned toward the door in unison and watched as Emily opened the door to admit the visitors.

Even though it had been only a few years since Keith last saw Gwain, in reality, several centuries had passed.

The man who entered the living room of Emily's house was older, but he had the same smile and twinkle in his eyes.

"Uncle Keith," he exclaimed as he entered the room and crossed the expanse between the door to where Keith stood in a minimum of steps. "I can't believe you're here. You'll never know how hard it was for me to ride away from you that day. You were the only father I ever really knew. I just had to follow my heart and it led me on the most incredible journey."

Chapter Fourteen

Scotland, three months later

The plane touched down in Inverness. After seventeen plus hours on the plane that made two stops after leaving Chicago, all three couples were in dire need of sleep. Ian was glad that they had accommodations waiting for them.

They arrived at the bed and breakfast that they'd rented for their stay in this, the capitol of the Highlands. From it, they could see the old castle, which was one of the few landmarks that Ian could identify.

Two weeks earlier, Ian had made Emily his wife in a double ceremony with Keith and Julie. Gwain and Denise had witnessed their unions in the county courthouse. It had taken him several days to convince Emily that the difference in their ages didn't matter and that he wanted a wife more than he wanted a non-committed lover.

The weddings had been a joyous occasion followed by an intimate reception for Emily and Julie's close friends and family. The wedding trip had been a gift from Gwain and Denise. It would be good to see Scotland again, even though they all knew there would be nothing that would remind them of home in the modern day country they once called home.

The next morning, feeling more rested, they had a Scottish breakfast with their hosts, before leaving for a day of sightseeing. Ian was anxious to see the area where he had spent so many hours trading in wool.

When they reached the wharfs where he had once had his office, he saw buildings were much too new to have been erected during his previous lifetime.

"Are ye looking for yer warehouse?" a familiar female voice asked.

Ian turned, as did Keith and Mac. To their surprise, Tabitha stood behind them. "How is it that you are here?" Mac asked, when the others remained speechless.

"Do ye think that I cannot travel through time whenever I wish? I have been watching the three of you and have been pleased to see that you have all found women to love. I have come to take you to the places you wish to see."

"Are you the woman responsible for bringing Mac to me?" Denise asked, putting voice to the question that Ian knew each of the women wanted to ask.

"Yes," Tabitha replied. "Just as I helped you to change places with Davida, I granted each of these men their wish to travel to the future. For Gwain, it was his undying love for you that promoted the trip. For Keith, it was his desire to be with the man he considered his son, and for Ian it was the love for his cousin that was behind his wish to journey across the centuries. I knew that Gwain would find love, but when both Keith and Ian found love as well, I was pleased."

"Whatever happened to Brenna MacIntyre and the children I gave her?" Ian asked.

Tabitha chuckled softly. "As a surrogate father, I didn't think you would be interested. The twins were both boys and they grew into great men. Together, they took over their father's manor and produced many children from each of their many wives. Like most of the children that you planted within the bodies of the young wives of Inverness, they were very fertile. You have many descendants among the great families of this area."

"I don't think I want to know about all those children," Emily teased. "Your days of being a surrogate father are ended, and I have the ring on my finger to prove it."

"The children don't matter, my love. I am told it would take all of my wealth to support a child, and then more. I have you and that is all I want in my life."

"And 'tis a wise man to know the proper words to speak to his lady," Tabitha commented, as she led the way to the building that now stood on the spot Ian's warehouse once occupied.

"This entire district was lost in a fire in 1530," Tabitha continued. "There were several deaths, including your manager who ran your business successfully after you disappeared. Had you stayed in this city, it would have been you who died in the fire. Since then, there have been many different buildings erected on this site."

Ian swallowed hard at the thought of the death of his trusted employee, Keith. He remembered turning over the business to him and telling him that he would not be back to Inverness. The man had been a good friend and the thought of such a horrible death brought a lump to Ian's throat. Knowing now that he was the son of Keith Fletcher made the loss even harder.

"I would like to see McGowan Manor," Mac said, changing the subject.

"Since your vehicle will hold all of you comfortably, you can drive there tomorrow. For today, I will leave you to discover the modern marvels of Inverness. I will meet you at the house where you are taking your lodging early tomorrow morning so that I can give you the directions to Grantown-On-Spey. That is the town that has grown up around what was once McGowan Manor."

"What of Fletcher Manor?" Keith asked.

"I prefer you save that until last," Tabitha confessed. "The descendants of your grandson have done well in returning it to a state that you will recognize immediately. For now, I will leave you to explore the remainder of Scotland on your own."

Before any of them could make further comment, the woman turned and walked away, leaving them to contemplate the fact that she had joined them and knew of all the history associated with the places that were of interest to them.

"There used to be an inn close by," Ian said, searching the street for any sign of something familiar. "I remember that I ate many meals there."

"It was probably destroyed in the fire that took much of this district," Mac commented.

Ian nodded in agreement. It was hard to think that everything he knew and remembered was gone, but over the years it was inevitable.

As they walked down the street, they found a quaint little pub and stopped in for a glass of ale and something to eat. Ian knew it was close to where his favorite inn once stood. If he was right, the house where he rented a flat would have been right across the street. By closing his eyes, he could see the entire street as it had been when he left over five hundred years earlier. Instead of the paved road, he could see the mud of the dirt street that ran in front of his warehouse.

"It's different, and yet I can see it as it once was," he finally declared.

* * * *

The next morning, using the directions given to them by Tabitha, they drove to Grantown-on-Spey. Ian and Mac were both surprised at the modern hamlet that had once been the village for the crofters who worked for McGowan Manor.

"I am anxious to see where the manor house once stood," Mac said, as a young man who resembled himself approached them.

"You must be a McGowan," the man said as he extended his hand in greeting. "My name is Angus McGowan. For what it's worth, I'm the lord of the manor, not that that means a great deal anymore. It's more of an honorary thing. Things aren't like they were in the old days, when the lord of the manor ruled over everyone in the area."

Mac nodded. He was glad that this man who was named for his Uncle Angus was not like Charles. There was only room for one high-handed lord of the manor for the McGowan clan in history. "I'm Mac McGowan from Wisconsin, in the United States," he replied. "This is my cousin, Ian Brice, and my uncle, Keith Fletcher."

"Don't forget us," Denise teased. "I'm Mac's wife, Denise, and this is Keith's wife, Julie, and of course Ian's wife, Emily. As much as I'd like to see the old manor house, I think we'd rather visit the shops. I'm positive we can find some great treasures."

Mac pulled Denise into a tight embrace. He knew that the manor house would bring back horrible memories of the man she called husband, laced with the beautiful memories of the nights when the two of them had worked so diligently to get her with child.

"I understand completely, love. We won't be long."

Together, the three of them followed Angus up the familiar path that led to the former home of both Gwain and Ian. To Mac's surprise, the manor house loomed in the distance, resembling the home he remembered.

"I'd expected to see ruins," he commented as they got closer.

"If you had come here ten years ago, that's what you would have seen. I was looking through the archives and saw what the original manor looked like. As I did, I told my wife that I wanted to restore it to what it once was. We had a meeting of the family and everyone agreed that the past was something that shouldn't be forgotten. Of course, once the restoration was completed, my wife insisted that we should install plumbing and electricity before we moved in."

Mac crossed the threshold and entered the great room where clan members once slept on the rushes and took their meals together. The room was still huge but instead of bug-infested rushes, the floors were covered with beautiful oriental carpets.

In what was once the kitchen with the fire-blackened hearth, shining stainless steel appliances were nestled against the walls that were made of stone, as though they were the original ones that once denoted the foundation of the house.

"This is the original foundation," Angus said, pointing to the stones. "I've even added an upper addition to look like the hand-drawn pictures that I found."

"It's remarkable, it's just as I remember," Mac said, his words hardly audible.

"As you remember it?" Angus asked.

"It's a long story and one that is probably lost to anyone in the family," Ian said.

"Ian Brice. That name is mentioned in the archives and you, Mac, look remarkably like the drawings we have of William. Is it possible that…no, of course it isn't, there is no such thing as time travel, is there?"

"If we can't tell family of our marvelous adventure, who can we tell, isn't that right, Gwain?" Ian asked.

Angus' face went white with the realization that the men who were mentioned only in family legend and rumored to have disappeared without a trace were standing right in front of him.

"You must spend the night here with us. I'm certain that what you have to tell us is best told to the entire family. My wife and I would be pleased if you were to be our guests."

"I guess it's up to the girls," Gwain said, "but I warn you these women will eventually take over the conversation. We had planned to find an inn here in the area before leaving for Aviemore and Fletcher Manor in the morning."

"Then we will save you the price of a night's lodging, and if my wife has anything to say about it, you will be staying longer than you originally planned."

* * * *

Denise knew that Julie and Emily were apprehensive about staying in the manor house where Ian had grown up and where Gwain had made delightful love to Davida so many centuries earlier.

For Denise, it was a return to a life she had lived for almost a year in 1470 as a young woman. As Davida, she had lost her virginity in a room that closely resembled the chamber where she and Gwain spent so many delightful nights perfecting their lovemaking.

"Do you remember the night you taught me the game of pain and pleasure?" she asked, when they had retired for the night.

"I remember it well, but I doubted that you would. It's been a long time since we engaged in anything that delightful."

"Are you saying that our lovemaking is not delightful, Mac McGowan?" Denise teased.

Mac grabbed her around the waist and kissed her with the passion they had shared when they were Gwain and Davida.

"This chamber demands that we should again try that delightful game we took part in so long ago," he said, as he pulled her nightgown over her head.

Shari Dare

"I like you naked and at my mercy," Mac said as he seated himself on the bed and pulled her down across his knees.

"You aren't really going to…" she began as he brought his hand down across her bare ass. "Oh my god, you are!" she exclaimed as he shoved his fingers first into her ass and then into her cunt. The feeling was so unexpected and pleasurable that she squealed with delight, as she had on the night Gwain first introduced the game to Davida.

Each time his hand connected with her ass, she anticipated him either putting his fingers inside her or massaging her clit until she came in his hand.

"At least you haven't lost your touch," she said, once they lay together in the big bed, preparing for more conventional lovemaking. "I'd forgotten how the pain and pleasure game aroused me."

"I had as well," he confessed. "It was being in this room that brought back the memory. I can't believe that Angus was able to reconstruct this house to look like the original."

"Considering all that has happened to us, it is entirely possible that he is the reincarnation of his namesake. Does he resemble your Uncle Angus?"

Gwain nodded. "I was thinking the same thing. Something tells me that Tabitha has had her hand in more things than time travel. At the time I traveled forward, she told me that she was immortal. I didn't believe her then but now I'm beginning to think that she was telling the truth. She hasn't time traveled to this time—she lives in it. It is entirely possible that she has been orchestrating the lives of all she has had contact with for centuries."

"I don't care if she is able to time travel or if she is indeed immortal. Without her, I never would have found you, lost you, and had you find me. For that I am eternally grateful. Now, let's stop talking about things that seem impossible but are staring us in the face. Instead, I would like to have you make love to me as you did to Davida all those years ago. I want to pretend that I am a virgin and the thought of you deflowering me is frightening."

Gwain straddled his wife and prepared to make delightful love to her throughout the night. As soon as he stuck his cock into her cunt, she

120

shrieked as though she was losing her virginity. When she did, he pumped harder, bringing her to the heights of pleasure.

Before ejaculating, he pulled back and began rubbing her clit in a circular motion. She squirmed beneath him as he made her come again and again in rapid succession. In this room, it was like the first night they were together. Nothing could ever take those memories away from her, especially after Gwain came to the twenty-first century to find her.

* * * *

They stayed at McGowan Manor for almost a week before the entire story about their time travel had been revealed to the clan. During that time, several journals had been produced that spoke of not only Gwain and Davida, but also Charles and his untimely death at the hand of his lover Brian. Even Ian and the time that he spent with the clan as a fosterling was recorded in great detail.

All of the journals, as well as the memories that were shared, made Keith anxious to see Fletcher Manor again. From everything he had heard, he would recognize it immediately.

On the morning of their departure, they left, armed with e-mail addresses that would help them to keep in touch once they returned to Wisconsin. The closeness they all felt to the McGowan clan made Keith wonder what they would find when he was once again at the family home he had lived in until he decided to go in search of his beloved nephew.

Unlike the long journey between McGowan Manor and Aviemore, it had been reduced to only a few hours by car. Between Keith and Mac, they didn't need the map that had been their constant companion during the trip to Grantown-on-Spey.

Keith was pleasantly surprised when he found the manor looking much like it had when he left. For him it had only been a little over a year ago, but of course over five hundred years had passed.

Without telling anyone who they were, they paid the admission for the open-air museum that it had become.

"Good afternoon, ladies and gentlemen," said a young man who greeted them. He was dressed in a kilt of Fletcher plaid. "You are about to take a walk back into history. A long-dead ancestor built this manor house in the thirteenth century. The last Fletcher to be lord of this manor and head of the clan was a man named Keith Fletcher, who disappeared without a trace in 1475."

The tour went on and Keith listened as their guide described the life he had lived before he decided to travel through time to find Julie. It made him sad to hear about the life that he lived as a young man. Of course, on the other hand, the fact that these people still remembered the man who had disappeared gave him great pleasure.

They spent the night at a quaint inn that they found in town. "Was it terrible hearing your past so vividly described?" Julie asked as they prepared for bed.

"There were good and bad moments. At times I wanted to grab that lad and tell him that I was Keith Fletcher. You don't know how hard it was not to be able to tell him the truth in the same way that Gwain and Ian told the people at McGowan Manor."

"I think I do, but I am pleased you didn't tell them. I doubt they would have been as understanding as the McGowan's were. I am pleased that I am one of the few people to know of your secret. Rather than dwell on it, I'd rather make love to you. Emily told me that Ian likes his cock and balls sucked, and that's what I have planned for tonight."

It took them little time to take off their clothes and prepare for a night of lovemaking. Once they were both naked, Julie pushed him down on the bed. With him prone and his legs spread eagle, she took his hard cock into her mouth and began to suck him until he came with great force. Emily had instructed her well, and she had waited until this special time to try her newfound skills on her husband. To her amazement, she enjoyed it as much as she knew he did.

When he spilled his seed, she began sucking on his balls until he begged her to stop. "Am I hurting you?"

"On the contrary, you make me happier than any man deserves to be. I cannot believe that you are the woman who, only weeks ago, feared sexual contact. Now let me pleasure you in the same way you have done me."

With a minimum of effort, he flipped her onto her back and began to suckle her clit. She moaned with delight and, like him, begged for the delightful torture to end so that they could make love in a more conventional way.

In compliance with her pleas, he mounted her and made love to her with a vengeance. Had she been younger, she knew that this lovemaking would have left her carrying his child. Instead, it warmed her heart in ways that she couldn't begin to describe.

* * * *

Their last night in Scotland was spent in Inverness. Ian no longer saw the city he once knew but the one that had grown to maturity during his absence.

They were staying at one of the many modern hotels rather than the bed and breakfast they had enjoyed when they first arrived. It didn't take him long to realize that this beautiful hotel sat on the same property that had once housed Athena's house of pleasures.

"On this very piece of land I was tutored in the art of love by Athena. She taught me how to love a woman."

"And I have been the grateful recipient of that knowledge."

"We will be making delightful love tonight, my dear. I know that you didn't want to marry again, but I am so pleased that you have agreed to be my wife. Now, we are going to spend our last night in this city, in the country of my birth, making love to each other. I plan to fuck you throughout the night, my little love slave."

He reached into his traveling bag and brought out the little whip that Emily brought to his condo on their second night together. He also handed her the harem girl costume and demanded that she put it on.

Once she was dressed in the sheer costume without the crotch, as well as the top that emphasized her ample breasts, he asked her to bend over. Seeing the white flesh of her perfect ass, he brought the whip down lightly across it. After he did, he caressed her clit before bringing the whip down again.

"Oh," Emily gasped, "that is delightful. I can hardly wait to use this little whip on you. What ever prompted you to bring it along?"

Ian smiled. "I read one of your erotic novels and realized that the whip might be fun to use. For tonight you are my slave, but when we get home, I will be your slave for the rest of our lives."

* * * *

The next morning, the three couples boarded the plane. Each of the women knew that they would always have a fondness for Scotland, and the fact that their husbands had crossed the barrier of time to find love in their arms.

For Denise, Gwain had come to find her and make her life complete. For Julie, Keith's quest to find his nephew had brought her pleasure that she never knew she could enjoy. For Emily, the promise Ian had made to his cousin had brought her a devoted love slave who would fulfill all of her sexual fantasies.

Life in Minter, Wisconsin would never be the same for any of them, nor would they have it any other way.

About the Author

Mild Mannered wife, mother and grandmother by day, Shari Dare spends her nights writing and writing and writing. Having been inspired by an English assignment in her sophomore year of high school, she had never quite finished the assignment. New stories pop into her head every day with never enough time to write them all.

A Wisconsin native, she grew up a country girl, but enjoys her "city" home. She and her husband of over 50 years, Bob, live in a mid-sized town close to the Illinois border. Deeming Bob "A Saint" for putting up with her she has never regretted marrying her high school sweetheart just two days after graduation in 1964.

http://www.derr-wille.com

Other Books by the author with Melange

Man in the Forest
Black Conley
Seducing Sir Gwain, Book 1 of the Gwain Series

www.ingramcontent.com/pod-product-compliance
Lightning Source LLC
Chambersburg PA
CBHW031834170626
46807CB00004B/1451